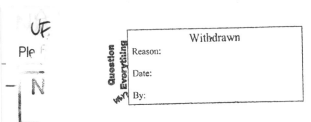

The Deliverance of Judson Cleet

Judson Cleet was a gunslinger of ill repute, going rapidly to seed, and when he hit Old Town in Texas all he was looking for was the next saloon, the next drink. What he found was trouble: trouble from men who attacked him for no possible reason and trouble from a young woman whose home was razed by fire and her husband hanged.

The trouble was still smouldering when renegade Texans camped on the Bravo and sat and waited. But it all exploded into fire and violence when a proud Mexican *ranchero* lost his cattle and daughter to the renegades who had decided the waiting was over.

Now it became a running battle with the rustlers driving the stolen herd. Could Judson Cleet, with the help of Marshal Sam Sloan, Chrissy Moran and Ramon, finally win his fight to right cruel wrongs and rediscover his destiny? Only time would tell!

The Deliverance of Judson Cleet

MATT LAIDLAW

A Black Horse Western

ROBERT HALE · LONDON

ISBN 0 7090 7300 3

Robert Hale Limited
Clerkenwell House
Clerkenwell Green
London EC1R OHT

Typeset by
Derek Doyle & Associates, Liverpool.
Printed and bound in Great Britain by
Antony Rowe Limited, Wiltshire

*Dedicated to my namesake and close relative,
the late Dr John Paxton Sheriff
of Dallas, Texas.*

Part One
Cleet Rides In

Chapter One

Judson Cleet expected trouble, and got it.

It seemed that the simple act of riding into a strange town – and God knew he'd ridden into plenty of them over the years – was enough to bring out from the woodwork the fellows who'd got calluses on their hands from practising fast draws and plugging rusty tin cans with hot lead. In his time he'd been challenged by scrawny kids with fluff on their chins and twisted rawhide thongs tying holsters to skinny thighs; unshaven town bums with greased-up six-guns stuffed into their torn pants, cheap alcohol on their breath and a crazed look in their bloodshot eyes; fancy Dans with natty pearl Stetsons and ivory butts to their shooters and a way of sneering down their nose that would have been laughable if it wasn't so damned dangerous.

In the sprawling settlement called Old Town, some way north of Laredo, it was none of these. Deceptively sleepy in the stifling heat, parched trees drooping among buildings that were crumbling adobe or

9

cracked, unpainted timber, it was a border town where trouble was a way of life, and trouble sneaked up on Cleet's blind side. It was, he supposed, a refreshing change – but, for God's sake, why? What the hell was it about him? What was it they saw? He was a grizzled has-been pushing fifty, with a rawboned stoop born out of weariness, and pale-blue eyes set in a permanent squint from the continual torment of the blistering south-western sun. His water canteen had long ago been exchanged for a whiskey bottle. The last time he'd hooked a gunbelt on the bony jut of his hips had been . . . aw, hell, now that *was* asking!

He'd ridden in as the evening sun rimmed the peaks of the Sierra Madre with fire, eaten his fill of tough beef and beans served by a pretty dark-haired girl at the café, then walked his horse across the wide, dusty square towards the pools of lamplight spilling from the slatted swing doors of the New Deal saloon. That early in the evening the place was quiet. He'd bellied up to the rough plank bar and ordered raw whiskey, swilled the rancid grease out of his back teeth with the first jolt and burned his vocal cords with the second. A hastily rolled cigarette compounded the damage so that for a while – what with the coughing from the harsh tobacco and the third stiff jolt tossed down to put out the fire – he was forced to knuckle tears from his eyes just to keep track of a bartender who was mostly standing still.

But that stage passed, and the evening crawled along. Swing doors slapped from time to time, letting in the cooling night air and men with desert-sized thirsts. The big room didn't exactly fill – in Old Town, that would have been a miracle – but there were enough people for decent conversation and the murmur of voices swelled to a satisfying hum. For a time, Cleet was conscious of bodies coming and going, one or two at a time, never enough of them to jostle him at the bar. Then a four-handed card game started up and, as the alcohol worked on the beef in his belly and its fumes pushed the world's troubles back behind a comforting mental numbness, he was vaguely aware of two men who came to the bar, stayed, paid him too much attention and stood too close for comfort.

Blurred senses or no, the survival instinct was still strong. These two looked like range riders, wore worn work garments and drooping felt hats, but the hickory butts of the pistols at their thighs were glossy with use, and in their eyes there was a look of . . . of nothing; just a hard blankness that told of a way of life with which Cleet had been all too familiar.

Most hardworking men walk into a saloon eager to shuck off the day's troubles. These two bore them like a massive weight on shoulders that were too tense, and a man like Cleet couldn't fail to notice that drinks were lifted by left hands leaving the right free for other business.

One man lurched close to jolt Cleet, and growled a curse. In the contact, Cleet caught the acrid tang of woodsmoke on the man's clothes, the stink of coal-oil, noted the smudges of soot on the hand resting on the

11

bar as he prudently kept his eyes lowered.

Maybe that was what caused the trouble. Maybe Cleet, drunk or not, had seen something he wasn't meant to, had begun instinctively to examine too closely certain feelings and impressions that on their own told him little about a man but, taken together . . .

And maybe the man with the blackened hand had seen more in Cleet's eyes than could be read in his own.

When the trouble came it was in the form of cold beer sloshing over Cleet as the sinewy arm holding the glass swung around, soaking his sleeve, darkening the front of his faded shirt and dripping from his belt buckle into the already damp sawdust. In the same instant, the other man standing at the bar cursed loudly and turned to slam him hard in the chest with the flat palm of his free hand.

Cleet staggered backwards, banged up against a shaky table with the back of his thighs, heard scrambling and a bottle fall and roll as he stared blearily at the two men who had stepped away from the bar to glare at him, those blank eyes cold in their hard, grinning faces.

And suddenly the hum of conversation in the New Deal saloon died away and all that could be heard was the wet, liquid dripping and the rasp of Cleet's breathing.

The man who had sworn at him, the lean *hombre* with dark stubble like a mask across the lower half of his lean face, was still holding a jolt glass in his black-gloved hand. Now he reached behind him to slam it on the bar, and stepped belligerently towards Cleet.

'Clumsy old fool, you just wasted a good glass of beer.'

Wearily, Cleet stepped away from the table. As the alcoholic haze was ripped apart by the hot winds of danger, he looked at the man's bunched fists, flapped a hand ineffectually up and down his soaked shirt front and said, 'I don't know how it happened, but let me buy your friend another—'

'I told you how it happened: you knocked his arm, you clumsy bastard—'

'No.' Cleet shook his head. 'That's not what happened.'

'You calling me a liar, old man?'

Cleet looked down at his glass. Somehow, he had held on to it, though it had tipped, slopping whiskey over his fist. Now, he wasn't sure if he wanted it. Perhaps he should get rid of it, return the favour in kind? He felt sick, knew he'd drunk too much, knew that for some reason these men were about to take advantage of that. And only then, as the seriousness of the situation began to sink in, did he wonder if one or both of them had seen in the drunken derelict a man they recognized and, in times long gone, might have had good reason to fear.

He looked across into the black button eyes of the impassive, mountainous barman and said, 'Give these gentlemen another drink.'

His answer was a clubbing blow thrown by the man

with the black-gloved fists. The hard fist took him on the side of the neck and, as his face went numb and his ears roared, the glass spun from his hand to scatter the men at the card table.

He hit the dirt floor awkwardly, shaking his head, cracking an elbow and tasting blood and sawdust as he tried to roll. Then both men stepped in, boots swinging. A hard toe slammed into the side of his knee. A hot bolt of pain shot clear to his hip as another boot narrowly missed his groin.

As he scrabbled backwards away from the driving, vicious kicks he looked up at the blank eyes, the glistening, set faces, and knew that this beating would end only with his death. And, though death was a state he had for some time contemplated with affection, now he was infuriated. He spat a curse. A kick grazed his shoulder. His head smacked against a table leg and he wriggled under the flimsy shield, felt sudden satisfaction as a wilder kick saw one man's shin strike hard wood. Then the table was sent flying. Wood splintered. Someone yelled a protest as a flying fragment clanged against a lamp and set it swinging.

Shadows swept back and forth across the floor, transforming Cleet's two attackers into grotesque giants who danced clumsily before his eyes. He was still moving backwards, using hands, heels, elbows, unable to rise because each such move was deliberately blocked. And now he was tiring, the unnatural posture and awkward movement putting too much strain on a body that had trained on raw whiskey and spent too many hours slouched in the saddle.

A kick cracked into his ribs, and the breath exploded from his body. Another nearly ripped his ear from his head, and he felt the hot wetness of blood. Agony brought tears to his eyes. He saw the two men through a shimmering mist, saw both men come in close to swing simultaneous kicks – and finish up in a tangle. As they bounced apart, momentarily off balance, Cleet rolled and came to his feet. He spun. The swing doors were behind him. A furious bellow of anger sent him plunging desperately through, into cool, sweet night air beneath soft skies and, as his boots echoed on the plank-walk, his arm was caught and held by a rawboned man on whose vest a badge glittered intermittently in the light winking with the slap, slap, slap of the swing doors.

Chapter Two

Cleet sat on the steps at the edge of the plank walk, elbows on knees, head in hands. Behind him, the New Deal had settled and was gently bubbling. Marshal Sam Sloan had continued on his rounds, well satisfied: two hard men had told him the reasons behind their indignation; a drunken drifter had been warned and pointed towards his horse; nobody had died.

The way of the world, Cleet thought ruefully; somebody had told him the meek would inherit, but he couldn't see that happening. The explanations had been one side of a story and probably lies, the marshal had accepted them without question, and the hard eyes that had continued to stare at him across the lawman had held a deadly promise.

Why? If they had set on him because of mistaken identity, who did they think he was? What was he supposed to have done, and when? Or was it the other way around? Had they been awaiting an arrival, mistaken him for that person and moved in to put a

17

stop to trouble he might cause in the future?

That would have made sense if he was a hired gunslinger brought in to help out in a range war. But, goddamn it, he was unmistakably a bum, a smooth-hipped drifter with watery eyes and course set for the nearest bar, and whatever he had been or might have been was well hidden beneath greying whiskers and a hand that trembled. Deliberately so, for Cleet's only desire was to pass through what was left of his life with the minimum of fuss.

'Easy, Rocky,' he said softly, as the horse at the rail stepped forward and flung its head.

Even if he'd come strutting in with six-guns flaunted and a swagger in his step, he'd have had nowhere to go, because in this corner of Texas a range war was about as likely as winter snow. The grassless plains and mesquite flats supported no grander enter-prise than the listless movement of horses and wet-back cattle across the waters of the Bravo, the only wars were the sporadic in-and-out skirmishes when bored Texans on the gather encountered sleepy Mexicans and disturbed their siesta.

'So we move on,' Cleet told the horse, and saw an ear flick, the light of the rising moon glint in an approving eye.

He stood stiffly, felt the pull of dry blood on his neck, the knife-pain that could be a cracked rib: shallow breathing was the order of the day, sudden movement not recommended. Knocked cold sober by the recent ruckus, still he went down the steps with the stumbling gait of the old drunk he was, flipped the reins free, swung with some difficulty into the saddle.

He crossed the wide street at an angle, moving into the rich smell of frying beef and onions issuing in warm billows from the open door of the café to torment the hungry horses at the rail, sniffing appreciatively because it would surely be some time before he again enjoyed the benefit of someone else's cooking. Yet even as he rode closer it seemed that the troubles that dogged him had not had their fill: wreathed in steam, a ghostly figure in the hazy yellow lamplight, the pretty girl who had earlier served his meal was standing just inside the doorway and, as Cleet reached the edge of the plankwalk, he saw a hand flash like a striking snake and slap the girl's face.

A low growl stirred in his chest. He swung Rocky, saw the girl stumble out on to the plankwalk as a big man with long greasy hair and a filthy apron came after her with his hand raised for a second strike.

'Enough,' Cleet called. 'Leave her alone.'

Two heads swung to look at him. In the girl's eyes he saw fright, then recognition and relief; in the man's irritation, then contempt.

'Ride on, feller,' the café owner said, 'unless you're part of this and want to get real gabby with the marshal?'

Cleet was down, loose-tying the horse. The girl was shaking her head, and he said, 'Part of what?'

'My takings are little enough,' said the big man, 'but your kind don't need much. If she dipped her hand in the cash tonight, she's done it before, and it could be you and her figure you've got a good thing going.'

'Did you?'

She looked numbly at Cleet and turned away from the big man. He grabbed for her arm. She shook him off, stumbled away along the plankwalk.

'You looked at her left hand?' Cleet said scornfully. 'She's a married woman, she'd have no time for the likes of me.'

'Still a thief,' said the big man, 'and good riddance.'

He spat into the dust, ran fingers through his greasy hair, and was gone. The girl had stopped some thirty yards away. As the café door rattled shut she began to walk back, and Cleet hesitated.

'You live nearby?'

Her face was pale. 'Far enough out to make the ride both ways near as long as time spent on the job.'

'And now there is no job?'

She shrugged.

'Will that make a difference?'

'You think I worked there for fun?'

'No, out of desperation. Ma'am, are you a widow?'

'I'm married to a man who thinks horse dealing will make him rich. He spends his time bringing stolen Mex' horses over the Bravo so they can get stole right back again.' With a sudden flash of spirit she said, 'I guess you could say dishonesty runs in the family, and we still ain't got the hang of it.'

He watched her untie a thin sorrel and swing into the saddle, waited until she had turned away from the rail and started down the street, then swung aboard Rocky and fell in alongside her.

They rode past the marshal's office as Sam Sloan was unlocking the door, caught the glint of his eyes as he intently watched them ride by. He's had some time to cogitate, and a second look, Cleet thought. Maybe now he'll have a brainstorm, hunt out those old Wanted dodgers. Get a bunch of mixed feelings if he comes up with the right ones, set behind his desk worrying if he was within an ace of glory or just plain lucky to be alive.

'I don't need your concern.'

'Ma'am, I'm just leaving town, same as you.'

She laughed ruefully. 'I can't believe this is happening. A man tries something on with me when business is slack, I slap him down and get accused of stealing, and all at once . . .'

He waited, saw the set of her jaw, the lift of her head, and said, 'And suddenly the town's low life reckons you're down to their level – is that what you mean?'

She was sensitive enough to flush prettily. 'I shouldn't even think that, because I don't know who you are, or what you are.'

'What I am is what you see. Who I am is Judson Cleet.' He waited, saw no sign that the name meant anything to her, and said, 'If that's what happened in there I should have stayed and taught that feller a lesson.'

'That's been done,' she said, and now her smile twin-

21

kled with amusement. 'When I said I slapped him down, I meant kicked – and right where it hurts.'

A bit jingled. A laugh rang out behind them, lost itself in the night. He knew she was watching him as they rode away from the lamplight of Old Town, knew that as those warm lights dimmed and the cold glimmer of the moon sent a shiver through the air she was glad of his company, yet at the same time nervous.

'Cleet?' she said, coming at him from a different angle. 'Should that name mean something?'

'Sam Sloan might dig something up.' He grinned across at her in the thin light. 'But it'll be ancient history on yellowed paper, and about as close to the truth as that story you told me.'

She let that slide – though her swift glance was as sharp as a knife thrust – and for a while they rode in silence, pushing north-west from Old Town and crossing the moonlit flats in the direction of the Bravo, occasionally turning aside to avoid stretches of tough of mesquite. Within half an hour they were close enough to smell the water. In another fifteen minutes, Cleet caught the tang of woodsmoke, and felt his scalp contract.

'You're welcome to stay the night,' she said at last, but even as he nodded his thanks he knew that her mind was elsewhere, her eyes never still.

'What is it?'

'I don't know.'

'Are we close?'

There was much taller mesquite ahead, gnarled

trees that blocked the horizon. But even their height couldn't hide the smoke smudging the moonlit skies, and once the smoke was seen the mind swiftly reached the conclusion that the faint glow visible through the tangled growth was not moonlight on water, but a smouldering fire.

And it was at that point that the girl dug in her heels and brought the thin sorrel to a reckless gallop and the remaining mile to her home was covered at a hair-raising pace that left Cleet trailing.

When he caught up with her – after a leisurely ride in to allow her some moments alone with the husband who stole horses for a living – he discovered that her breakneck ride to join the young maverick had achieved its purpose, but ended in untold grief.

Chapter Three

They'd chopped a clearing out of the tough mesquite and built their house with a view across a long slope to the oily flow of the Bravo and the distant, majestic Sierra Madre. But in the few short hours since the sun had gone down behind the mountains, someone had undone all their good work. A fierce fire fuelled by black coal-oil had destroyed timber walls, furniture and belongings, the only thing left standing was a magnificent stone chimney over which the builder must have sweated time and blood, and around that monument to his endeavours an irregular mound of glowing ash was almost liquid as its colours shifted and changed in the night's gentle breeze.

By razing the house, the marauders had opened up to the young woman who rode up to that scene of destruction a clear and terrible view of the depths of their wickedness: against the trees beyond the smouldering wood ash that had once been a home they had selected a stout, horizontal bough and from that limb they had hanged her man.

Cleet rode past the ruins with a heavy heart. The young woman who had outdistanced him over those last several hundred yards was down on her knees, sitting back on her heels, rocking. She was bent forward, her long dark hair trailing silkily as she cupped her face in her hands. Her husband's boot-heels swung and rotated lazily just inches above her head.

In a silence it was sacrilege to disturb, Cleet nudged his horse forward and went around the woman. The dead man's hip nudged his shoulder. He stood in the creaking stirrups, reached into his pocket for his clasp knife.

'Ma'am.'

She looked up, wet-faced, then hastily moved back. Under Cleet's hand the rope was as taut as an iron bar. He was forced to hack with the sharp blade. The fibres parted suddenly with the snap of finality that seemed to signify the end of a young man's life. But it was illusory. Life had long been extinguished; the man was dead as he spun lazily at the end of the rope, dead as he fell, dead when he hit the ground and crumpled.

The girl moaned. Cleet stepped out of the saddle and for the second time left her to her sorrow. In outbuildings the marauders had left untorched at the edge of the timber, he found a spade. In half an hour he had dug a grave at the edge of the trees where she indicated, and after another fifteen minutes he was standing in silence alongside her in front of the mound of dark, fresh earth as she bowed her head and whispered broken words that were not for his ears.

And all the while, his shirt damp with cooling sweat, Cleet was remembering, and listening for distant sounds that might herald danger. He and the girl had separately marked their short stay in Old Town with altercations that were angry, and violent, and their departure had surely been observed by the mildly interested citizens of the town, and others with bleak eyes and their minds set on murder. For if the men with the stink of woodsmoke on their clothing had been calculated in their attack on him, they would follow it up. Instinct put Cleet on his guard, made him edgy. He was standing alongside a girl whose husband, she told him, moved stolen horses across the Bravo, and that didn't seem enough reason to hang a man, burn down his home and go hunting a complete stranger.

'What now?' Cleet said.

'Now nothing. Pete's dead, and I . . .' She broke off, coughed as the acrid smoke caught at her throat, and he saw her swallow, fighting the tears. 'He had his faults, Lord knows, didn't always treat me right. But he was my husband, and now. . . .'

'Pete?'

'Pete Moran. I'm Chrissy.' She shrugged. 'That's it. No relatives on either side. I guess all that's left for me is to return to Old Town, make money any way I can.' From under long lashes her eyes met his, and he knew what she meant and thought of the paint and powder on the sporting girls he'd encountered in saloons and cantinas in the hard border towns, and emphatically shook his head.

'That's not for you. Besides, you're getting ahead of yourself. Your place was burned down for a reason. If we find out why, we'll know who. Then those men can be made to pay.'

Her laugh was short, bitter.

'You think I can fight them on my own?'

He hesitated, then shook his head. 'No. That's Sam Sloan's job.'

'The lawman? Aren't you forgetting I've been run out of town for stealing?'

He watched her climb on to the thin sorrel, and said, 'That feller in the café can be made to tell the truth. And even as it stands, a misdemeanour doesn't alter the seriousness of what happened here.' He gathered Rocky's reins, swung into the saddle, eased the horse alongside the girl. 'Where are you going, Chrissy?'

'Forget it, Cleet, ride on, leave me be. I'll get by.'

'Maybe it's me I'm worried about. I got dragged into this at the bar in the New Deal. Sure, I could turn my back, ride on to the next town, the next saloon. A couple of hours ago, this fine horse I'm riding had convinced me that's what I should do. Now . . .'

'You listen to a horse?'

'I—'

Abruptly, he leaned across and touched her arm in silent warning.

'What—?'

And then she, too, heard the soft, swelling beat of hooves, rapidly approaching, and her hand went to her mouth and her eyes met his, wide with fear.

'There's time for us to get clear,' Cleet said, and squeezed her arm.

After burying Pete Moran they had moved away from the trees, putting the smouldering ruins of the house between the girl and the heart-rending sight of her husband's grave. Now, Cleet led the way back, cutting through the acrid white smoke that was drifting across the clearing, deliberately taking the horses through the mess of cut sods and fresh dug earth on the far side so that hoofprints would be lost.

Then they moved into the trees.

He took them deep, worrying little about the sharp crackling of dead twigs and the snapping of fresh branches, for the approaching riders would have the thunder of hooves and the wind in their ears. They moved away from the river, and before long Cleet saw ahead of him through the trees moonlight on open country and knew they had traversed the broad stand of tall mesquite and had reached the other side. Far enough. Still under cover, but with the trees scattered and grass underfoot and a clear run ahead of them if flight became necessary.

'You're unarmed.'

'Am I?'

'I noticed, in town. If these men find us, we won't stand a chance.'

'Who are they, Chrissy?'

'They're . . .'

Cleet was down off his horse, hand light on the saddle, looking back the way they had come. Nothing could be seen. Searching eyes were baffled by moonlight filtering weakly through the trees. Staring into the maze of tangled undergrowth made a man dizzy.

'Chrissy?'

'I don't *know* who they are. Why should I?'

But that wasn't what she'd been about to say. He waited. Nothing was forthcoming, so he said, 'No warnings? Nobody rode up, suggested to Pete this might happen if he kept moving stolen horses?'

'Come on, Cleet. Pete wasn't making enough cash to keep us in food. A blowfly would have annoyed them more.'

'Them?'

'Yes. Whoever burned down our spread,' she said wearily. 'Them.'

'If Pete was so small-time,' Cleet said, 'this doesn't make sense.'

'I'm telling the truth.'

Cleet nodded absently, aware of the sudden silence, his mind skipping across the expanse of mesquite to visualize the scene at the burnt cabin. If he was right, two men would be watchful in the saddle, their cold eyes taking in the moonlit scene, their ears listening for the faintest sound. Those two men with six-guns tied low and the stink of woodsmoke on their clothing and a man's death on their conscience, had expected the girl to ride home, had planned it that way so that the shock and fear of what she would find there would put her to flight.

But Cleet was the unexpected. The more he thought about it, the more it seemed likely that somebody had witnessed the brutal hanging of Pete Moran, and been seen. In Old Town, soaking up liquor at the bar, Cleet was the stranger who stood out and maybe had dark visions he was trying to drown. The two men had attacked him because if they were right then they would remove a dangerous witness, if they were wrong, well, Cleet was a bum over whom nobody would grieve. Then, after Sam Sloan had stepped in to halt the fracas, the killers had seen Cleet cross the street to talk to Chrissy Moran, and watched the two of them leave town together.

'No,' Cleet said, 'you're not telling the truth.'

He registered her quick protest, but again he was listening to the sound of hoofbeats, now moving away, and he turned to the girl, the tension leaking out of his muscles as he lifted a hand to stem the flow of hot words.

'I'm right, you know I am, but you can tell me your story another time. It looks like the killers have given up for the night, but they've got sharp ears and right now it's too dangerous to move. You can use my blankets . . .'

Suddenly she was desperately weary. He felt her dull eyes on him, watching numbly as he unstrapped his blanket roll. Then she slid from the saddle and clung to the horn while he gathered dry brush and spread his slicker and blanket on the makeshift mattress.

She lay down without a murmur, drawing the blanket up to her chin. Cleet moved away, built a hearth from rocks and lit a small, smokeless fire. In no time he had coffee bubbling over the tiny, crackling blaze, the rich aroma masking the stink of the burning house that drifted through the woods, but when he poured some into his only cup and carried it to her, she was asleep.

A troubled sleep? Oh yes, for this grief-stricken young woman had ridden from Old Town to find her house in ashes and her dead husband hanging from a tree and it seemed that, ahead of her, life offered nothing but an aching emptiness, a future as daunting and bleak as the desert landscape.

But why this sudden explosion of violence? And why would Texans hang a fellow countryman for stealing scrawny Mexican horses? It didn't make sense. Pete Moran *must* have been playing a deeper game and, if so, then Chrissy knew more than she was admitting to. When Cleet had asked her who could have done this terrible thing, she had almost blurted out names, then stepped back from the brink. If she knew that much – and he was convinced that she did – it was likely that she would know why Cleet was now a marked man.

And if that reason was linked to the deadly game that had cost Moran his life, then the two men who had come after Cleet would not rest until he was dead.

Cleet watched the sleeping girl in silence for several moments, experiencing an unexpected wave of tenderness at the sight of the soft hair falling over her cheek and the dampness of unshed tears on dark eyelashes.

Then he turned away. He drank the coffee, tossed away the dregs, stripped the rigs from the horses and fixed hobbles, then placed his saddle against the bole of a tree. For a moment he hesitated, gnawing at the side of his lip, his eyes distant, remembering, despairing: how many empty years, how many dusty miles, how many shabby towns – and how many times had he lain on that blanket and looked up at the stars and sworn that the old Judson Cleet was gone, never to return?

And now this. A stricken young girl. A dead man in a cold grave. And two others with guns tied low and the bleak eyes of hunters.

Cleet took a breath, held it, let it out soft and slow through flared nostrils. All of that, and nothing explained – and he was too tired to think. There was a dull ache behind his eyes, the after effects of too much bad alcohol. He lifted a hand to his forehead, rubbed its centre gently with fingers that had the faintest of tremors. Then he unbuckled his saddle-bag, took out a bundle wrapped in oilskin, and unrolled it.

In the moonlight, the two bone-handled six-guns in the worn gunbelt gleamed with a cold and deadly fire.

Chapter Four

They came back in the cold hours before dawn, riding out of the open country beyond the mesquite like black shadows racing before a storm. Muzzle flashes were the lightning that lit up the trees. The crackle of their pistols were puny rolls of thunder deadly enough to kill.

As Cleet's head jerked from the saddle and he rolled blearily away from the chill comfort of his leafy bed to stagger to his feet, his mind was already racing. Not yet dawn, still a deceptive half light with the new day a faint pink streak across the wide horizon – but he and the girl had been found. How? And even as bullets snickered through the trees and he pulled both bone-handled six-guns free and tossed the belt aside, his eyes had picked out the reason: their hobbled horses, silhouettes against the light, innocently wandering away from the trees now but clearly visible to marauders.

Behind him soft movements, then gasps of bewildered shock as Chrissy came fully awake.

'Stay there – and keep down!'

The two men were on them.

Cleet snapped a shot, heard a squeal of fright and saw a horse rear, front legs pawing. The gunman leaped clear, landed cat-like, returned Cleet's shot. The other man was also out of the saddle. He slapped his mount to send it trotting clear then, with six-guns blazing, advanced on the timber in a low, weaving crouch.

And suddenly it was as if the long-silent six-guns that were unfamiliar hunks of metal in Cleet's hands had come alive.

In the cold air of early morning his head was clear. The tremor of the previous night was gone from his fingers. The bone butts of the Colts were snug in his palms. He stood erect, his eyes remote yet focused, and with precise up and down movements of his forearms, thumbs and forefingers he repeatedly lifted, cocked, aimed and fired each pistol in turn. But the aiming was instinctive, the alternate movements so blindingly fast that the crackle of the separate shots blurred into a fusillade, became a volley that numbed the senses and overwhelmed the attackers.

When Cleet began firing, each Colt held six bullets. In the space of as many seconds both pistols were empty, their tilted muzzles silently leaking wisps of smoke. On the edge of the mesquite, two men lay dead.

'My God!'

Her voice was at his shoulder, tremulous, disbelieving.

'Don't look,' Cleet said, and even to his own ears his voice had altered. It was as if by taking up his six-guns he had invested in a worn-out, drunken bum the hardness of cold steel. It was something he had vowed never to do – for in past years those guns had earned him an infamous reputation – yet there could be no denying that in breaking that vow he had become a powerful force that had seen good triumph over evil.

But this was just a beginning. As Judson Cleet found his gunbelt in the carpet of dead leaves, pouched the still hot six-guns and began the messy business of lifting two dead bodies and lashing them belly-down over their saddles, he knew that he had taken the first irrevocable step towards an unknown destination. It was possible that the young widow was familiar with the trail, and knew what lay at its end – but she would not tell him. Or, not so far. If Cleet had been asked for an opinion, he would have said that her indebtedness to him might bring about a change of mind. But her face was set as she assisted him in his grisly work, her eyes held a wariness that was close to fear, and Cleet's mouth clamped into a grim line as he recognized the signs: the vow had been broken; he must now face the consequences, both good and bad.

And he could make that easier by staying on the right side of the law.

'We'll take them into town,' he said, when the grim work was done. 'Hand these two fellers over to Sam Sloan.'

'You don't need me for that.'

37

'Without you, there would be no killing. I think you should discuss that with Sloan.' He waited, got no reaction and said, 'In the light of what happened in the saloon, this could look bad for me.'

'All right.' She shrugged. 'We'll both tell him what's happened. But there's nothing Sloan can do.'

'About what? You're coming up with bits and pieces of a story that don't add up. And if not Sloan, who then?'

She pursed stubborn lips, shook her head.

'Who were they, Chrissy?'

'I told you, I don't know.'

'Sloan might not accept that.'

'That's not my concern.'

'What is? What was Pete doing to rile somebody so bad they stretched his neck?'

Without answering she turned away, bent to her saddle and swung it over her horse, her lips tight as she worked at the cinch.

Cleet shrugged. He saddled Rocky, keeping a wary eye on the two gunmen's horses that stood with the whites of their eyes showing, nostrils flaring as they sniffed the fresh blood.

They were ready quickly, coffee pot packed away – gunbelt again deep in a saddle-bag – blanket-roll tied behind the cantle, hearth-stones scattered and fresh dirt kicked over the fire's still warm embers. In ten minutes they were on their way, the two horses carrying the dead gunmen taking up the rear, and in that time the pink streak on the horizon had become a flaring sheet of livid flame that cast long shadows across the irregular landscape and brought with it the first hint of a warmth that would rapidly develop into the blistering heat of a South Texas day.

Old Town was stirring when they passed the town's empty cattle pens and rode in. An aproned swamper was out in front of the New Deal, splashing soapy water. The general store's doors were wide open. A pregnant woman was talking to a heavy man in dusty broadcloth and a white apron, both of them standing on the store's gallery.

Heads turned at the sound of the approaching horses. Cleet saw the woman's hand go to her mouth as she caught sight of the two bodies flopping limply in death. The big man took a step towards the approaching riders, then turned, looked towards the jail, and yelled.

By the time Cleet and the girl had tied up at the rail, a boy had been summoned by the black-clad banker and was racing across the square, and Sam Sloan was out in front of the jail, and waiting.

His expressionless blue eyes were fixed on Cleet. One eyebrow was fractionally cocked. Can't make it out, Cleet thought, and allowed himself an inward smile. He's looking at the same feller he got out of trouble, a drunken bum who was getting kicked into the street, only now the two men who were doing the kicking are belly-down – and there's not a pistol in sight.

'Leave them there, they'll be taken care of,' Sloan said as Cleet swung down. 'Step inside, both of you.'

The jail was solid, big for a small town, the adobe bleached white by the sun. The big office was dusty, motes drifting like fine summer rain in the sun slanting through the open door. Barred windows were set either side of the door, and high up in the side walls. The room was sparsely furnished with roll-top desk, chairs, an iron safe, a pot-bellied stove. A stone archway with a door set in strap-steel bars led to the cell area, where a table and chairs beneath a hanging oil lamp were set centrally on the dirt floor between the empty cells that lined three walls.

Sloan gestured to chairs, waited until they were seated then sank into the swivel chair behind the desk. He tilted, swivelled lazily, then tipped his hat back with a stiff forefinger to expose crisp grey hair.

'I guess I had you figured wrong,' he said to Cleet – and waited.

He was a man, Cleet decided, who scattered lengthy pauses in his conversation like buckets waiting to be filled.

'Depends,' Cleet said.

'On?'

'On how you had me figured,' Cleet said.

Sloan sighed. 'Don't try my patience, Cleet,' he said, and Cleet realized, with some misgivings, that he had picked on the wrong reason for the marshal's cocked eyebrow. As he'd anticipated, Sloan had checked through the pile of curling Wanted dodgers on the end of his desk and come up with the name. Maybe he was still in the dark about recent happenings, but he sure as hell knew some hard facts about Cleet's past and, because of that, had been taken aback by Cleet's gall in returning to Old Town.

'You kill those two waddies?'

'Waddies?' Cleet smiled cynically, and nodded. 'Sure. With good reason.'

'It needs to be,' Sloan said. 'You know who they are?'

'I know what they've done.'

Sloan ran a finger across the dust filming his desk, looked at the scored line, wiped his finger on his shirt.

'There's a man called Lupe Waggoner,' he said, watching Cleet. 'Came through town a couple of month ago, brought half-a-dozen tough *hombres* with him. Rode up the Bravo a ways, been camped there ever since. So far, he ain't bothered with a house.'

'Then he's not staying,' Cleet said, and frowned. 'Are you telling me the two men I shot worked for Waggoner? And that I should know this feller's name?'

'Burke and Riley,' Sloan said. 'Waddies, like I said. What you might call Waggoner's soft underbelly. The rest of his crew think cowpokes are rope-twirling sissies.'

'Whatever you might think, these two were no different. Waggoner gave them orders to put this young woman's house to the torch, hang her husband from the nearest tree.'

'You saw them do that?'

'No.'

'What about you, ma'am?'

'I was in town.'

Sloan nodded. 'Both of you were.' He looked at Cleet, shook his head. 'You shot them dead to get even for what happened earlier, ain't that the truth? Figured dead men don't talk, so it'd be easy to pin this crime on them.' His eyes had hardened, hiding his thoughts. 'Where'd it happen, this hangin'?'

'I took Chrissy home only to see the dying fire through the trees, helped put her husband to rest. We were about finished when we heard riders.'

'Goddamn!' Sloan swore softly, irritably. 'You heard riders! But you didn't see them. And you're telling me that was Burke and Riley?'

'Who else?'

Sloan snorted. 'All right, maybe it was them. I saw all four of you leave town, you two first, the other two maybe fifteen minutes later. But they were riding in the same direction, that's all they were doing. Heading for Waggoner's camp on the Bravo. They were going home, Cleet.'

'If so,' Cleet said, 'they got lost. They hung around and attacked us before first light, without warning.'

'I swear that's the truth,' Chrissy said. 'If Cleet hadn't been there . . .'

'Last night in the New Deal,' Cleet said, 'they stunk of woodsmoke and coal-oil, had soot smeared on their hands, deliberately picked a fight—'

'Why?'

'I rode down the Bravo from Eagle Pass, saw Waggoner's camp from a distance, must have passed the Moran place further downriver at the wrong time.'

Cleet shrugged. 'If they saw me out there, recognized me when they came into town . . .'

He broke off as a wagon came to a rattling halt outside the jail, turned to glance narrow-eyed into the dazzling sunlight beyond the open door where a bearded man was already down off the wagon's seat and untying the first of the dead men. Sloan came from behind the desk, crossed the room and stepped outside. Voices murmured. Cleet listened hard, but couldn't hear what was said. When Sloan returned, his expression was unchanged.

He pushed the door to and, standing with his back to it, said, 'Maybe things happened like you say, maybe you're telling the truth – but given your background, you can understand why I'm a mite suspicious.'

'If he can,' Chrissy Moran said, 'I can't. I don't care about the man's past. I was with him from the time he walked across from the saloon. If he's a liar, so am I.'

Sloan grunted. His back was turned as he looked out of the window alongside the door. 'All right, ma'am, let's say I take your word for it: Burke and Riley attacked you and Cleet. The fire and the hanging, well' – he turned quickly and held up his hand as she opened her mouth – 'ma'am, it's not even hearsay, both of you are pinning the blame on those two fellers for what they did before and after – and that ain't right.'

He spread his hands, shook his head and pulled a wry face, then walked round his desk and took a gunbelt down from a wall hook. 'Nevertheless, I've got to admit that in the light of what happened there's two questions need answering. The first is, why would *anyone* burn down your house, hang your husband?' Leather snapped as he buckled on the gunbelt, settled the heavy holster on his thigh. 'Second is, why would Lupe Waggoner be the man to do it?'

'Ride out and ask him,' Cleet said tightly.

'No need,' Sam Sloan said. 'He's comin' across the street right now – and he don't look too happy.'

Chapter Five

In the silence that was thick and heavy in the office, a fly buzzed weakly, dying in the heat.

A Mexican slouched lazily against the wall, battered sombrero tilted forward, one eye milk-white and blind, a scar cutting diagonally from one eyebrow across a stubbled cheek to split and distort the ragged moustache. Two six-guns pulled fancy gunbelts into tight loops hanging from slim hips. A Winchester dangled from a gloved hand.

Alongside the Mexican, his gringo partner gazed hard at Cleet with eyes as pale as a cougar's. He was fleshless and angular, a man with loose joints and bony hands and an aura of silent menace. His black outfit was white with dust. His single pistol was high on his left hip, tilted, butt forward.

Both gunmen stood against the wall near the office door, detached but watchful.

Lupe Waggoner, tall, hook-nosed, a man of fifty with chill blue eyes and a lean frame like sprung steel, had

hooked a chair with his foot and now sat near the desk.
Sam Sloan had settled in his swivel chair. One of his
six-guns was on the desk in front of him, within easy
reach of his right hand. He looked as lazy as a
rattlesnake basking in the sun.

'He says what?' said Waggoner, gaunt face register-
ing disbelief.

'Your men, Burke and Riley, attacked them.'

'Also,' Chrissy Moran said, 'they burned down my
house and hanged my husband.'

She was staunch, unflinching. Cleet had expected a
flood of tears as time passed and shock wore off and
the full realization of what had occurred hit hard.
Instead, her courage left him filled with admiration.

'Those are damn lies,' Waggoner said.

'No, these things happened,' said Sloan.

'You believe him?'

'I believe her,' Sloan said, and flicked her a warning
glance.

Waggoner's eyes glittered. 'I heard about the fracas
in the saloon. All right, it looks like Burke and Riley
couldn't leave well alone.' He shrugged, jerked a thumb
at Cleet. 'They picked the wrong man, paid the price. It
happens all the time. But they had no reason to burn
down this young woman's home.'

'Now who's lying?' Chrissy said. Her face was pale,
her eyes blazing.

'Ma'am,' Sam Sloan said, 'if you know the reason
why your husband was killed, let's all hear it.'

'Could be it's a mite risky,' Judson Cleet said.

'Whatever it is, it drove men to commit murder, and Chrissy could be next. Maybe it'd be best if you hear about it in private.'

Waggoner shook his head, for the first time looking directly at Cleet.

'No. It's my men accused of the crime. I want to know why.'

'Your men are dead,' Cleet said. 'The finger's pointing at you.'

'Jesus!' Lupe Waggoner said, starting forward in his chair and glaring across the desk at the marshal. 'Do I have to take this lip from a gunslinger wanted across six states?'

'Cleet's got a point,' Sloan said – and waited.

Cleet grinned.

Waggoner narrowed his eyes, fumed, cursed softly under his breath. 'Goddammit, I've got a right to know,' he said. There was no answer. Sloan waited; Cleet was still grinning.

Waggoner came up out of the chair, kicked it backwards. He stepped forward, placed both hands flat on the desk, thrust his Lupe-like face at Sloan.

'Understand this: my men are dead. If they committed a crime, I had nothing to do with it. And it died with them. It's over. Finished.'

With a final, ferocious glare at Cleet, he thrust away from the desk and headed for the door. All three men clattered out into the sunlight and started across the street. The door stayed open, letting in dust and heat.

After a moment, Sloan said, 'For a man who wants

to distance himself from what happened, he was surely showing uncommon interest.' He shook his head, turned to Chrissy and said, 'Ma'am, you have something to tell me.'

Chrissy looked at Cleet. He shrugged, knowing she was aware that she had refused to give him the information, and was now willing to give it to another man. He spread his hands palm up and smiled his forgiveness.

'My husband was a Texas Ranger,' she said softly, and Sloan blinked.

'I had him down as a man moving halfway worthless horses back and to across the river so's he could lose money,' he said. 'What the hell – begging your pardon – was a Ranger doing in this neck of the woods?'

'Pete wanted to settle down. We . . . we had marriage problems because he was always off somewhere chasing renegades or keeping Indians and settlers apart.The move here was meant to bring us closer together, but he was too good a Ranger.' She swallowed, looking damp-eyed at unpleasant memories. 'There's a wealthy Mexican rancher called Rivera, friendly with the Captain of Rangers in Austin. He's always been willing to lose a few head of cattle from his big herds to raiders from across the river. Marks them down as wetback losses. But he's aware that Texans are moving large numbers of cattle north to the railheads in Kansas. And his *vaqueros* have reported happenings on this side of the river that have made him suspicious.'

Sloan was tilted back, rocking, his head nodding slowly as he mused, eyes half closed. 'I know Diego Rivera. He got nervous around '67 – I know that because it's something we discussed. And a couple of months ago, the situation gets serious for Rivera when a feller moves in accompanied by men with hands ain't done any hard work and belts heavy with pistols,' he said slowly. 'This feller camps on the Bravo, then sets back in the shade and appears to go to sleep.'

Chrissy nodded. 'Now Rivera is thinking of putting night guards on his herds,' she said. 'He *knows* something's up. He sent to Austin for help some time back, and although Pete was at first reluctant, he was in the area and when word came he kinda drifted into it.'

'Your husband moving horses was just something to do so he wouldn't look suspicious?'

'With Diego Rivera's backing. Gave Pete a reason for being both sides of the border. He claimed that a good long view from different angles gave him a clearer picture of what was going on.'

Sloan dragged open a drawer, tossed a Bull Durham sack on to the desk, slid it towards Cleet. From a rack under the desk's roll top he took a blackened corn-cob pipe, struck a match, puffed smoke into the hot air.

'Did the clear picture tell him anything about Lupe Waggoner?'

'Nothing he could take to Austin, or bring to you. But Pete was on to him from the day he arrived.'

Cleet rolled a smoke, lit up, sat back, waiting for the next, inevitable question. A feller with a young wife,

49

struggling to get established, doing his damnedest to make a living selling sway-back horses. That's the impression he'd have given to almost everyone who knew him – yet, somehow, he met a violent death.

'If your husband was keeping his Ranger duties under his hat,' Sloan said, 'how come Waggoner – if it was him – cottoned on to what he was doing and got rid of him?'

Chrissy's eyes were haunted in a suddenly pale face. 'I talked to a lot of people when I was working in the café. That's what I was supposed to do: I took the job to talk, listen, pick up information. I can't believe it, but I must have let something slip, and if I did then I'm responsible—'

'No.' Cleet reached across, squeezed her arm. His tone was emphatic. 'You wouldn't have done that. This happened because men like Waggoner can smell danger. If Pete risked a ride upriver—'

'He did, more than once. Sometimes I went with him.' She met Cleet's eyes, and in her own a glimmer of mockery lurked. 'I guess I was laughing at you when those two men attacked and you told me to keep my head down. I carried a pistol, rode alongside Pete. . . .'

'Then you were both reckless, and he was unlucky. One way or another, he was spotted by Waggoner's men.'

'A wild bunch,' Sloan said. He took the pipe out of his mouth, stabbed it at the far wall as if the two gunmen were still slouching there and said, 'Those two, Diaz, Van Haan, are always with Waggoner. There's half a dozen more've ridden into town a couple of times. Caused no trouble, but I figure that's because they're under strict orders. I wondered what the hell was going on. Now, well, if you're right, ma'am . . .'

Cleet was sceptical. 'A drive north, a thousand miles or more with a bunch of gunslingers nursemaiding Mexican cattle?'

Sloan looked at Cleet. 'Yeah, I know. It don't make sense.'

'So what's Waggoner up to?'

'With stockyards, and no cattle.'

'And gunslingers,' Cleet said, 'but no cowpokes.'

They let it rest there. The talking had dragged on, with very little achieved. Chrissy stood up, yawned politely into the back of her hand with what Cleet guessed was nervous exhaustion, then walked over to the door and stepped out into the bright sunlight. Cleet killed his cigarette, eased his shoulders. As far as he was concerned, his involvement was over. He'd buried the girl's husband, brought two dead men into town, told his story. The whys and the wherefores never had been his concern. What happened next was up to Sam Sloan, but . . .

Cleet stood up.

'You taking this any further?'

Sloan had risen, and was shuffling papers. 'Go after Waggoner? If he does something, maybe . . .' He shrugged.

'What about the county sheriff? Why not drop it in his lap?'

Sloan grinned. 'Political ambitions. Over at Austin most of the time, lickin' boots.'

'What about me?'

'You're free to go. I'm a small town lawman, too stupid to recognize in a drunken bum the infamous outlaw known as J.C. Cleet. And this business was self defence, ain't that right?'

Cleet nodded. He wandered over to the door, stepped outside. Chrissy was at the hitch rail, looking lost. The square was dazzling white after the shade of the office. Cleet felt the heat beating down, almost taking his breath away. He took another step.

Then something hit him a powerful blow in the chest and he was knocked backwards, body falling away from legs that refused to move until he floated off into a blackness that was like an unending night without moon or stars and nothing to hear but an echoing crack that faded into silence.

Pain.

A hammer blow of pure agony, sending his breath whistling through his teeth as his eyes snapped open. Vision and sound blurred then, after furious blinking, uncannily clear.

Water tinkled. Metal clinked. Sunlight slanted across a hanging oil lamp thick with dust, glistened on the sweat filming the plump face of the man bending over him. Thin hair plastered across a mottled brown scalp. Glasses perched on the end of a fat nose. Behind them alert, faded blue eyes that flicked to meet his, then away.

Murmured words. Then movement: a hand, fingers and thumb clamped either side of his mouth, forcing it open, a second coming across and suddenly the sour taste of old leather as a hard strip was pushed between his teeth.

Then the flicker of light on a sharp blade, a white bolt of agony that arched his back and clamped his teeth on the thick leather belt as the groan at the back of his throat threatened to become a scream that he fought to contain as metal grated on metal—

Blackness.

Cleet came out of the second period of unconsciousness with a clear head and a dull ache gnawing at his left shoulder. He opened his eyes, blinked in the dusty sunlight; turned his head gingerly, then with more confidence as the ache remained bearable, and realized that he'd been moved from the table onto a cot in one of the cells at the back of Old Town's jail.

The cell door was open. If he'd had breath to spare, he'd have let it out in a sigh of relief.

Beneath him, the cornhusk mattress rustled as he swung his legs sideways and sat up. His head swam. Nausea welled up, and he swallowed noisily. Then the giddiness faded, the cell steadied, and he recalled the terrible blow in the upper part of his chest, the periods of agony, the concerned face looking down at him. Concerned, or confident? He touched his shoulder, felt the firmess of clean bandages, and managed a grin. Confident or not, the old boy had done a good job. Or maybe the feller with the rifle had helped him by being out in his aim. A couple of inches to the right . . .

And, yes, it had to be a rifle, Cleet thought, planting his feet and standing up. He'd been looking straight across the wide square. As far as he could recall, there was nobody within sixty feet of him. The buildings opposite? Well, there was the livery barn – and if he was to put the blame on Waggoner and his crew, that was as likely a spot as any for them to have waited in the shadows. The advantage was all theirs. He'd walked out into blinding sunlight. The gunman had picked him off like a sitting duck on a stall at a county fair.

Now the balance was tipped the other way. When the rifle cracked, the gunman would have watched Cleet drop, then turned and run. He'd figure him for dead. That gave Cleet the advantage. But did he need one? Hadn't he already decided that this fight was not his? And didn't this slug in the chest enforce the view that the quicker he put miles between him and Old Town the better it would be?

He walked unsteadily out of the cell, reached to his top pocket for tobacco then remembered they'd taken off his shirt. He grinned weakly, and went through the stone arch into the office. Sloan was in his swivel chair, feet on the desk. He eyed Cleet, nodded approvingly.

'Jensen said you'd be as good as new.'

'The doc?' Cleet shook his head. 'I owe him some thanks, but for good as new I'd have to reclaim too many wasted years.'

'On the performance of the past twelve hours, you're doing fine.'

There was something indefinable in the town marshal's tone that nevertheless whispered an urgent warning to Cleet. Alerted – but not knowing to what – he sat down, took the balled-up shirt Sloan handed him and scowled ruefully at the bloodstains.

'Where's Chrissy?'

'She wanted to ride on,' Sloan said. 'But when I asked where, she had no answer. Maud Gibbs, wife of Henry Gibbs the store owner, took her across the street and got her fixed up in the rooming-house. I had a few strong words with Bannion over at the café, and she's there now eating a late breakfast.' He watched Cleet for a few seconds, then said, 'Are you going to play with that, or put it on?'

Cleet shook the shirt open with his right hand. It flapped, caught the bright light slanting through the high windows, and he blinked and looked at Sloan.

'What the hell's that?'

'Deputy's badge.'

'You out of your mind?'

'In Old Town, even with one arm,' Sloan said, 'you're the best man for the job.'

His jaw tight, Cleet began to unpin the badge.

'Leave it!'

'The hell I will.'

'You will – or you go back in that cell, and this time I'll lock the door.'

'For what? Killing in self-defence? Saving a young

girl's life? You told me I could walk away, I step outside and take a slug in the chest, now this—'

'Look through those dodgers. Take your pick from five or six of 'em over the years, maybe more, I ain't counted. But I know the most favourable'll still get you twenty-five years in the Pen, the worst – and there's several – will see you sharing Pete Moran's fate.'

Cleet felt the breath whistling through his nostrils, his pulse racing, a tremor in the hands holding the shirt that was not weakness, but anger. He glared at Sloan, at the litter of Wanted dodgers on the desk, felt the weight of endless years of life on the wrong side of the law and knew he was beaten – for now.

Awkwardly, he thrust an arm into the shirt, swung away when Sloan leant across to help, slipped the shirt on unaided and buttoned it. He stood up to tuck the shirt into his pants. When he looked down, the badge pinned to material made dark and stiff by his own blood glinted mockingly.

He looked up. Sloan still hadn't moved, hadn't shifted his feet from the desk.

'All right,' Cleet said, 'I'm a deputy. So now what?'

Chapter Six

Blue smoke from the camp-fire drifted across the flat banks of the river known as the Rio Bravo del Norte to the Mexicans, the Rio Grande to Texans, colouring the thin white mist that was rising to blanket the water. The night was cool and still. Firelight danced on the canopy of leaves and flickered on men's faces, a tin pot rattled as a hand reached into the flames and the aroma of strong java cut through the scent of woodsmoke, and a harmonica was a haunting sound outside the circle of light.

'He's dead.'

'You know that for sure?'

Hunkered down by the fire, the Mexican, Diaz, grinned, his teeth flashing, milk-white eye staring blindly at the night.

'Across the square, in daylight? I see him clear, take my time with the shot. You think I miss?'

'I think J.C. Cleet's a hard man to kill.'

It was Lupe Waggoner who had reached into the

flames to take the hot coffee pot in his gloved hand and pour the scalding, smoky liquid into a battered tin cup. He drank, dragged a hand across his lips, shook his head and squinted into the darkness away from the fire.

'You were there, Johnny,' he called. 'How'd it look?'

'He's dead. He was caught cold, walked into Diaz's slug.'

Van Haan's voice was flat, final – and disgruntled. The gaunt gunslinger was a long black shape lying some yards away on a blanket spread over his yellow slicker, his hands behind his head which rested on the saddle pushed up against the bole of a tree. To his right, another man was asleep with his blanket over his face, gunbelt resting on the carpet of dead leaves.

For some time Van Haan's tuneless whistle had accompanied the reedy sound of the harmonica but now, as the player segued from 'Dixie' into 'When Johnny Comes Marching Home', he scrambled to his feet and walked menacingly over to the fire.

'Tell that bastard to quit,' he growled at Waggoner, 'or I'll knock that goddamn harp down his throat.'

'Purty tunes, Johnny. Leave the kid alone.'

Diaz spat hissing into the fire. 'Johnny Van Haan is thinking of the bayous back in Louisiana,' he said, 'but he cannot go there because he went so loco, one time, he up and plugged his ma and pa.'

'You too, Diaz,' Van Haan growled. 'Shut up or take your chance.'

'Anytime,' Diaz said amiably.

'Both of you save your energy for Mexico,' Waggoner said.

And from beside the tree the man with the blanket over his face mumbled, 'Will you three for Christ's sake shut up and let a man sleep!'

'Is all right, Concho,' Diaz said with deep irony. 'Van Haan is always full of hot air, but he has blustered and thrown down his challenge and now he is finished.'

'Hah!' Van Haan found a cup in the black ash at the edge of the fire, tipped it upright with his boot and poured coffee, then looked at Waggoner. 'And what the hell's all this about Mexico? We've been settin' here for more than a month. You told us all about Rivera's herds but I reckon you're playin' some kind of joke on us, and I tell you now, Lupe, it's wearin' pretty thin—'

'You know damn well why we held off.'

'Sure.' Van Haan's eyes flashed in the firelight. 'And I was against it. One man, a slip of a girl, what could they do?'

'What about Cleet? You don't think he was part of it?'

'Cleet rode through by chance. Hell, I know that worn out shootist of old.'

'And now Johnny is again muy loco,' Diaz said, eyes glittering. 'He wanted Cleet for himself, but I pull the trigger and with one bullet—'

'Let it be!' With a twist of the wrist Waggoner flung coffee dregs into the fire, sending sparks and smoke hissing at the startled Mexican. 'Tell me, what date is it now?'

'Who the hell knows, May, maybe?' Van Haan glared at Diaz, wrapped his bandanna around his hand and gingerly picked the hot cup out of the ashes. 'End of May, right?'

Waggoner nodded. 'Right. And what was it you told me? You didn't come along to nursemaid a couple of thousand stinkin' Mex' cows all the way to Kansas?'

'Said it, and meant every word.'

'Well, if we've got our dates right, Court Blane's due in Old Town any day now.'

'With wads of cash to pay for cows we ain't got.' Van Haan's tone was caustic.

'And enough top hands to take 'em to Kansas when we do get them.'

Van Haan looked at Waggoner over the cup's rim. 'That right? We rustle Rivera's cattle, hand them over to Blane and his men – and that's it? One night's work, we get paid?'

'Not quite. Blane'll want protection. I figure we take him as far as the Red, stop short of the Nations, then drop back and spend some cash in Fort Worth.' He looked questioningly at Van Haan. 'How's it sound?'

'Better every minute.'

'Then listen to this. Soon as Blane rides in, we'll decide when we move. With luck, I reckon tomorrow afternoon.'

'In daylight?'

'Sure. The way we're workin' it, ain't no reason not to. Blane's 'punchers move the cattle, bring them across the river. You four watch their backs, deal with any *vaqueros* get hot-headed.' Waggoner grinned. 'But there'll be no trouble, I guarantee it.'

'Seems to me,' Diaz said, 'we tasted your guarantees that time we pulled the bank job in El Paso. As I recall, we rode away from there without one single dollar bill, and Van Haan with his hide perforated.'

Waggoner glanced across at the nodding Van Haan, and shook his head. 'This time, there's no doubt: we take those cattle without a shot being fired.'

Across the fire, Diaz had narrowed his eyes. 'And if Sam Sloan gets wind of this thing we do, he turns up maybe with a posse and we have *vaqueros* at our backs, *gringos* in front—'

'No pursuit,' Waggoner said smoothly, and grinned. 'No Sam Sloan. I guarantee it.'

'OK, we see.' Diaz shrugged, then squinted at Waggoner. 'And you, my friend? When all this is going on, when we are out there taking Rivera's cattle with all these guarantees protecting us from *vaqueros* and *gringo* posses – where are you, my friend?'

'Hell,' Waggoner said, throwing down the tin cup and moving away from the fire, 'I'll be right here with Court Blane, looking after the slice of insurance that'll make those guarantees secure – and that means before you go chasing after Mex cows, I've got a job for you and Van Haan.'

Chapter Seven

After leaving the jail with his bloodstained shirt on and his badge glittering in the sunshine, Cleet took an easy stroll across to the café and spent a little time talking to Chrissy Moran. She was drawn and subdued and, although Cleet tried to draw her out, he knew that she was troubled about her situation. She was a young woman who had been struggling to keep her marriage together and seen it snatched away from her. Weighed down by grief, she could not bring herself to think beyond the present, and the present was grim.

Cleet tried to cheer her up, but the nagging ache in his shoulder made him aware that he was merely going through the motions. Finally, he left her with a promise to talk again soon, and took himself with considerable effort to the rooming-house and booked in.

He slept for eighteen hours.

The next day Cleet and Sloan left Old Town when the sun was already high and hot, and an hour later splashed their horses into the Bravo in a sparkling shower of spray that cooled Cleet's forehead and dampened the shirt that had, for the past ten miles, rubbed irritatingly against the bandages covering his wound. Then the horses were swimming, the cold, muddy water was up to Cleet's waist and his breath went with a painful gasp so that he was forced to grasp the horn with one hand and cling on. As they pushed the horses up the far bank, Rocky slipped on the wet mud. The jolt sent pain knifing through Cleet's shoulder, and he cursed softly under his breath.

Sloan caught the sound and glanced back, but said nothing until they had cut across a stretch of open grassland and drawn rein in the scant shade of a thin stand of cottonwoods. Then he said, 'It's all easy going from here, Deputy, and you'll find Rivera sympathetic, and a gentleman.'

He was right on all three counts.

The Sierra Nevada was a high smudge across the horizon, shimmering in the heat-haze ahead of them as they pushed west. But the terrain they traversed was rich grassland, dotted with cattle, and in the far distance they could see *vaqueros* rounding them up into groups that were being brought together to be driven to the ranch for the summer matanza, or for the stockyards. The land was mostly flat with gentle, sweeping undulations, and although Cleet could feel the weakness like a heavy weight within him, he had no difficulty keeping pace with Sloan until the imposing single-storey ranch emerged like a floating mirage from the haze and they trotted into a wide yard.

Don Diego Rivera met them halfway. He was, Sloan had told Cleet earlier, an elegant Mexican *ranchero* who was proud of the fine, tile-roofed adobe buildings of Buena Vista that he had inherited from his father, prouder still of the thriving cattle business he had helped his father establish and, through shrewd dealing, increased ten-fold in value since the old man died. But now he was angry. Sloan knew him well and paid him occasional visits and, on one of them, the *ranchero* had told him how he had heard of the cattle drives that began in '67, and had guessed shrewdly that it would be a matter of time before some enterprising Texan cast an eye across the border into Mexico where herds of cattle roamed free and virtually unguarded. True, many of them were worthless. But Rivera's were well fed and watered, some 5,000 head of prime beef on the hoof that would fetch a good price even after a long, arduous drive north.

And Don Diego Rivera, Sloan told Cleet, was a man of high principles with the unblinking patience of a hovering bird of prey. He'd wait and he'd watch, and go on watching and waiting, but when the one careless move came, he would pounce – and if that move threatened his family . . .

'Let me guess,' Rivera said, as the lawman swung down from the saddle. 'You are here about a man called Lupe Waggoner. So, what has happened, has he made a move, shown his hand?'

'Not in any way that affects you, Don Diego,' Sloan

said. He waited for Cleet, introduced him to Rivera and, when the two men had shaken hands, said, 'Cleet took a slug in the shoulder that was likely dispatched by one of Waggoner's men.' He shook his head. 'That's the good news. The bad is, that Ranger who was sniffing around, poked his nose in the wrong place and ended up dangling from the end of a rope.'

Rivera's face was bleak. 'He was a fine boy. My *vaqueros* knew of Waggoner, though not of his intentions—'

'We still don't know for sure,' Sloan cut in, but Rivera shook his head and dismissed the idea with a sweep of his hand.

'Pete Moran had no doubts. It was he who warned me. When I expressed concern, he told me to talk to my friend in Austin, ask for help.' He smiled crookedly. 'I think that boy was bored, keen for some action – and now you tell me he is dead.'

'Left a wife, too,' Cleet said, and saw Rivera's swift, perceptive glance as his voice emerged as a dry croak.

'I am thoughtless,' he said. 'I have not yet formally welcomed you to Buena Vista; you are injured, and I am keeping you standing out here in the hot sun.' He touched Cleet's arm, then turned and led the way across the yard towards the house, and Cleet saw an Indian woman taking fresh baked bread from the horno and Mexican ranch hands going about their business with that deceptive slowness that nevertheless gets everything done on time. Horses dozed in a sturdy corral of slick peeled poles on the far side of the cluster of low buildings, and some way beyond that, shrouded in dust as they filled with cattle, an extensive range of pens.

As they neared the house, a young woman came out. She was dressed in an elegant riding outfit, topped and tailed by a flat black hat and glossy boots.

'I'm off,' she said to Rivera and, with a flashing smile as the men tipped their hats, she walked gracefully across the yard towards the corral.

'My daughter, Maria,' Rivera said, and for an instant his dark eyes glowed with pride, and love.

Then they were through the heavy wooden door set in five foot thick walls and in the dim coolness of a living-room, and Cleet had in his hand a cup of water cold enough to pain his throat as he drank. He drained it, felt the ice-cold liquid at once send new life coursing through his veins, and returned the empty cup to the small man of immense age who had brought it to him, and now took it back with a gentle smile.

He heard Rivera murmur, 'Gracias, Octavio,' and caught the old man's almost imperceptible bow as he left the room. Sloan was already seated. Rivera motioned Cleet to a settee of rich leather. He sat with some difficulty, relaxed against the cool leather – favouring his left side – and watched Rivera light a thin cigar. The *ranchero* blew a stream of smoke, then spread his hands gracefully.

'So, Sam Sloan,' he said. 'I am delighted to welcome you again to Buena Vista, and I extend that same welcome to you, Mr Cleet.' He nodded to both men,

67

then went on, 'I welcome you despite the bad news you bring – but what now? For example, do you have anything new to tell me?'

Judson Cleet's words, echoed by the Mexican *ranchero*. Sloan smiled, and said, 'Well, a helluva lot's happened, but I still don't know what Waggoner's playin' at so nothing's changed. Leastwise, not for our benefit.'

'True. With the Texas Ranger dead it is Waggoner who is better off. He now knows one man can no longer do him harm; a pair of eyes can do no more watching.'

'But if you look at it from another angle, him believing he can now move freely could work in our favour,' Sloan said, and glanced pointedly at Cleet.

Cleet was doubtful. 'You figure I'm your hole card?' He pulled a face. 'One of those two gunslingers pulled the trigger, watched me drop, then lit out. He'll figure I'm dead, sure, which seems to give us an advantage. I'd already figured that out – but so what? I'm a bum who happened to be in the wrong place. Me being out of the way ain't cause for celebration.'

'You heard Waggoner,' Sloan said. 'He knows your reputation.'

Rivera's black eyes gleamed. 'You are a skilful shootist, Señor Cleet?'

'The best,' said Sam Sloan.

'That's not the term,' said Cleet, 'that most folk would apply to a killer.'

Sloan shook his head. 'I'm satisfied that's in the

68

past. Far as I'm concerned you're a deputy, working on my side of the fence.'

'To what end?' Though his head had cleared, Cleet still couldn't understand Lupe Waggoner's game, or his own use as Sloan's deputy. 'The Ranger's killers are both dead, and there's no way of showing Waggoner gave the order. That leaves us with a man settin' in a temporary camp on the Bravo. Is that a reason to arrest him?'

'No,' Rivera said, frowning at the tip of his cigar. 'But if he is there for a while, apparently doing nothing, is it not highly suspicious?' He flicked a glance at Cleet, one eyebrow raised.

'Yeah,' Cleet said, 'but if we confront him with that argument he'll tell us he's about to set up in the cattle business or some such, then sit back and laugh himself sick while we try to prove it can't be done.'

'So we let him alone,' Sloan said. 'I'll lay odds every one of his hands is drawing fighting wages. He's waiting for something, and it looks to me like the only thing we can do is wait him out.'

'One dark night,' Rivera said, emphasizing the point with a stab of his cigar, 'he and his men will cross the river, gun down my *vaqueros* and steal my cattle. I know what he has been waiting for. He has been waiting for my *vaqueros* to bring the cattle into one place. When they are here, in my pens – then Waggoner will move. This is what Pete Moran told me – and I believed him.'

'All right, if he does that, then what?' Sloan said. 'If

he outguns your men, he's got a couple of thousand head of stolen cattle. What does he do, drive north with those same men who gunned down your *vaqueros*? Hell, they'll muddle through getting them as far as the river, but most gunnies don't know one end of a steer from the other.'

'And around we go in circles,' Cleet said, 'gettin' nowhere. Don Diego, we already talked our way to that point back in Old Town, and got bogged down with nary an answer. Waggoner can steal your cattle and move them a few miles, but he can't make the long drive to Kansas with a handful of gunslingers. Unless you can come up with some ideas. . . .'

'Impossible,' Rivera said. 'The situation is clear, you are right, and I am at a loss.'

'Then arm your *vaqueros*,' Sloan said. 'Double your night guards, if you have the men, make sure they ride in pairs and keep their eyes and ears open.'

Rivera nodded. 'I have done that,' he said. 'And although my talk suggests I have given up hope, that is not the case. My men are numerous, and loyal. Who is to say that they cannot beat Waggoner and his desperadoes? It is one thing to ride into a ranch and drive away two or three thousand head of penned cattle, but it is another matter entirely to try that when a number of determined men are filling the air with hot lead.'

'And Waggoner's only got a handful of men,' Cleet mused.

'He had more,' Sam Sloan said to Rivera, 'but Cleet

plugged the two could have been responsible for the Ranger's killing.'

'You see?' Rivera's eyes were bright. 'Already he is outnumbered – and it has already been pointed out that his men are shootists and will have little knowledge of how to move large numbers of cattle.'

He glanced happily at Sam Sloan and with a rare, flashing smile, said, 'And, if I must resign myself to doing battle with thieves and in the meantime am unable to come up with any more good ideas of my own, then the least I can do is to offer you some fine wine to compensate for your wasted journey.'

They spent another pleasant hour with the Mexican *ranchero*. Then, warmed and mellowed by the aged wine, they mounted up and pointed their horses away from Buena Vista and back towards the border. As far as Cleet could make out, they'd achieved nothing. Sloan had warned the wealthy cattleman to be extra vigilant and to make sure all his night riders were armed and alert to danger, and that was the best he could do. But, Cleet mused, when gunslingers of the calibre of Diaz and Van Haan were around, that was like giving small boys handfuls of pebbles to fight off full-grown bullies armed with rocks.

The *ranchero* was doing everything he could to prepare for trouble – but what the hell was Lupe Waggoner playing at?

Rivera had made the point: he had been warned by Pete Moran that when his cattle pens were full,

71

Waggoner would make his move. The crux of the matter was how he made that move. If Waggoner wanted cattle, he must cross the border into Mexico. He could do that legally by paying a fair price. But if that was his intention, why was he waiting, and where were the 'punchers he would need for the long drive?

With answers other than the obvious one offered by Rivera still eluding both men, they crossed the river and approached Old Town, skirting the empty cattle pens that in better times had been constructed in hope but through the apathy of a declining population were now decaying with disuse. Eyeing them, Cleet gave voice to his thoughts and said, 'I can't make out if I'm dizzy with too much wine and sun, or too much think-ing – but I know, whatever the damn reason, I'm gettin' nowhere in figurin' out Waggoner's intentions.'

'But you're interested?'

Cleet flashed Sloan a glance. In the marshal's eyes he saw approval, and a hint of satisfaction, and Cleet was astute enough to understand the reason.

'I guess what you mean is, pinnin' a badge on my shirt and giving me something to think about gave an old drunken bum back his self-respect?'

'And a purpose in life,' Sloan said. 'Don Diego's a fine man and I'm beginning to believe that, if theft is Waggoner's intention, he's biting off more than he can chew. But if he does succeed, it'll be up to you and me to put things right, in which case I'll have done what I'm paid to do, and you'll have taken a small step on the long road to atonement.'

72

'Big word,' Cleet said, 'but if it means what I think it means, I agree with those sentiments. However, I hate to take away the credit,' he said after some moments' thought, 'but I reckon Chrissy Moran got to me first and pointed me down that long road. There ain't nothing like the look in a young woman's eyes to make a man take a long hard look at himself and—'

He broke off, because Sloan was no longer listening. While talking they had turned into Old Town, and started across the square towards the jail. But the marshal's eyes had been drawn towards the saloon. A dozen jaded horses were standing hip-shot at the hitch rail. Half-a-dozen men in trail-soiled clothes were sprawling on the edge of the plankwalk with Stetsons tipped back and glasses in their hands. Enough noise came billowing through the swing doors to suggest as many again were inside.

And as Cleet followed Sloan and swung down outside the jail he saw, cutting across the square towards them, two men whose apparel and demeanour stamped them as bosses.

A cattle outfit was in town. But where was the herd?

Chapter Eight

The burly man with the white Stetson and fancy tooled boots stripped off a tan leather glove and stuck out his hand.

'Court Blane,' he said to Sloan as they shook. His gaze was penetrating, his demeanour – in Cleet's instant assessment – deliberately overpowering. Blane released Sloan's hand, replaced his glove and nodded towards the second man, a lean, big-boned character with a dragoon moustache and pale-blue eyes. 'My straw boss, Jack Clayton.'

'Sam Sloan,' Sloan said. 'The feller lookin' a mite sickly is my deputy, Judson Cleet.'

Blane nodded. 'We saw you two fellers ride in all badged up, figured you'd like to know what's going on.'

Sloan glanced with amusement at Cleet, and nodded. 'That's mighty decent of you, Blane,' he said – and waited.

The four men were outside the jail where they had come together. Cleet looked across the wide square to the shadowy, yawning entrance to the livery barn and, remembering the bullet that had slammed into him, instinctively reached up to rub his shoulder. Clayton wandered away to the hitch rail, fondled Cleet's horse, then rested his hands on the rail and spat into the dust. The sun beat down. The still air smelt of horses and dust and hot, dry timber. A ripple of laughter issued from the saloon. Cleet listened to Court Blane's deep, confident voice, and frowned. The man was talking, but not making sense.

'I've brought a dozen top hands,' Blane was saying. 'They're whooping it up, but I figure they're entitled to fun after the ride from Houston. And they'll be out of here by nightfall, that's a promise.'

'Houston, you say?'

Blane nodded. 'A long ride, but I'm a businessman and I follow the money.'

Sloan deliberately looked about him at the empty, sun-baked square, the run-down buildings, then back at Blane. 'You follow the money? To Old Town?'

The big man laughed. 'Passing through,' he said. 'I've got almost five thousand head of cattle waiting for me upriver. Cash on the hoof. We'll drive them east to pick up the Chisholm trail at San Anton', the big pay day comes some months later in Ellsworth, Kansas. But first, there's the small matter of a remuda.'

Sloan's face was expressionless. 'Why don't we step inside the office and talk?'

Clayton turned from the hitch rail to catch Blane's eye. 'Unless you need me, I'll head back to the saloon.'

'Fine, Jack,' Blane said and, as the rawboned fore-man strode away, he followed Sloan into the jail.

Cleet went after them more slowly, the weakness still troubling him. Sloan was behind his desk, Blane in a straight chair fishing a cigar out of his shirt pocket. Cleet hooked a chair with his toe and took it into the deep shadows away from the slanting sunlight where he sat down with considerable relief.

Sloan was already posing one of a number of obvious questions.

'Have you paid for these cattle, Blane?'

'Cash. Handed it over to my business associate and representative almost three months ago.'

'And you've been in touch with him since then?'

'From time to time.'

'Has he got a name, this associate?'

Blane was becoming impatient. 'Waggoner,' he said. 'But something tells me you know that, so what the hell's going on?'

'You say you're taking your hands upriver tonight?'

'That's right, but—'

'When you do, Mr Blane, you'll find that Waggoner has got himself some men who prefer six-guns to lass-ropes, but precious few cattle.'

The cattleman's jaw tightened.

'What do you mean by precious few?'

'None.'

'That's hard to believe.' Blane glared at Sloan, looked with irritation at the still unlit cigar, poked it back into his pocket. 'Waggoner wired me from Laredo just a couple of weeks ago. He told me—'

'I can guess what he told you,' Sloan said, 'but at that time you were still in Houston.' He looked across the room at Cleet. 'When did you say you rode down from Eagle Pass?'

'Yesterday.'

Sloan spread his hands and shrugged. 'Yesterday, Mr Blane – and nary a cow to be seen.'

'Then I don't know what's going on.'

'Would you like me to tell you?'

'Half-baked theories to blacken a man's name? I don't think I would.' Blane stood up, made as if to walk out, then turned back. 'Waggoner will have an expla-nation. He's a man I trust. If there's a story to tell, he'll tell it—'

He broke off as Cleet laughed softly, and for a brief, tense moment, Cleet thought the big man was angry enough to walk over and throw a punch.

Sloan had tipped his chair back and was smiling crookedly. He said, 'Oh, I'm sure Waggoner can tell some tales. Could be they'd have something to do with how his men walked out of here and, not too long after, Cleet took a slug in the shoulder. Could be you'll have to break the news to them that the shot wasn't fatal, and the man they thought dead is now wearing a badge.' He teetered lazily. 'Diaz and Van Haan – those names mean anything to you?

Blane shook his head impatiently. 'Nothing. And you'll recall I mentioned a remuda. Waggoner will come up with the cattle, I guarantee it, and for the drive north my men need horses.'

'Looking for good horses for sale around Old Town would be like fishing for trout in the desert,' Sloan said. 'Best place to try is over the border. Cross the river, head due west, first spread you hit is owned by a man called Rivera.'

Blane hesitated, then nodded, and now there was something in his eyes that to Cleet, from clear across the room, suggested the old *ranchero*'s name had rung a warning bell.

'Thank you, I'll do that,' Blane said. He swung away with his back stiff and his face set and walked out into the sun.

Cleet eased out of the chair, stretched gingerly, looked a silent question at Sloan.

The marshal grinned. 'Old Diego'll be happy to sell him as many horses as he needs. And forewarned is forearmed: if the old buzzard doesn't put two and two together while he's making some easy cash, I'll eat my hat.'

'D'you notice how Rivera's name hit Blane?'

Sloan shrugged, reached for his pipe. 'Sure jolted him. But it could be he's on the level, gave Waggoner the cash in good faith expecting him to buy cattle from Diego, and can't figure out why it ain't happened.'

'You know that's unlikely.'

'About as unlikely as rain falling in the next couple of months. But he's said his piece and gets the benefit of the doubt.'

'Like Waggoner?'

'Yeah, Waggoner's got it until he makes a move. We think his men plugged you – but thinkin' ain't knowin'.'

'But we know he's after Rivera's cattle. That makes him a rogue, and Court Blane's no fool. My guess is he's in deep with Waggoner. Talk of cash is hogwash. He wants those cattle the easy way so that every dollar he makes in Kansas is profit.'

'I'll reserve judgement.'

'But in the next few days all hell could break loose. You don't seem concerned.'

Tamping tobacco into the bowl of his pipe with his thumb, Sloan gestured vaguely.

'I'm concerned, all right, and I figure, like me, you're capable of working out what's bubblin' away on the stove.' He fired up, puffed smoke, watched Cleet sit in the chair vacated by Blane and scrape it around so he could gaze out of the door and across the square. 'Two men back in Houston got together and planned a cattle drive. They figured Old Town would be a good place to start: fifty or so inhabitants, a town marshal with his work cut out just to stay awake, a county sheriff miles away and with his sights set on governor. All adds up to a sleepy town within spittin' distance of the southern end of the Chisholm.'

'But no cattle.'

'You saw Blane's reaction to Rivera's name. He knew of him, all right, and was pissed that I brought him up. Rivera's essential to their plans; without his cattle, there's no drive.' Sloan rubbed the warm bowl of his pipe against the side of his nose, absently buffed the greasy wood with his thumb. 'So one of the men came on ahead with a bunch of *mal hombres*, a month or so later the other feller follows, expecting to see cattle ready to move. Only something made the first feller hold back.'

'Moran?'

'Well, Rivera ain't finished his round-up, which makes stealing a couple of thousand head a mite difficult. But, yes, Moran too, and what he represented.'

'Texas Rangers.'

'Right. Was the kid alone? Or did he have partners watching his back? And watching Waggoner?' Sloan sucked at his pipe and nodded slowly, satisfied with his thinking. 'Until Waggoner knew the answer, he couldn't make a move.'

'And then,' Cleet said, 'I rode in.'

Sloan grinned. 'Cat among the pigeons. You rode down the river looking like a drunken bum but with your eyes everywhere. Another Ranger on the prowl, Waggoner figured. And he made up his mind.'

'Had Moran murdered, rode into town for a look-see, saw his chance to try for me.' Still gazing across the dazzling brightness of the square he said, 'What were those two fellers called?'

'Diaz, Van Haan.'

'Yeah, I thought I knew that mean Texan. Crossed him years ago. Walked into a poker game over at San Angelo, caught a young kid cheating, shot him dead when he kicked the table over and went for his gun.'

81

Cleet shook his head. 'Johnny Van Haan's brother.'

'Where was Van Haan?'

'Right there. Too much whiskey'd slowed him down. He swore he'd make me pay, sometime, somewhere.'

'That bother you?'

'Not right then. But later. . . .'

Sloan waited, and Cleet saw the man's blue eyes and sensed the workings of a shrewd mind that missed little.

'That same night a cowpoke in town to get rid of year's wages as fast as he could, owned up to being the cheat. Turned out I'd killed the wrong man.'

'Jesus! And after that?'

Cleet pursed his lips. 'Let's say the effect of Van Haan's promise and the realization of what I'd done wearied me enough to make me take a hard look at my life, change my ways.'

'And that was difficult?'

Cleet smiled crookedly. 'You saw me when Burke and Riley were having their fun in the saloon. It's been a long ride, mostly downhill.' He shrugged dismissively. 'Anyway, the point I was about to make is the one we made to Rivera: with those two dead, Waggoner's short-handed. But he's still got Diaz and Van Haan, a couple more gunslingers on the payroll, and Waggoner's as mean and dangerous as any two of them.' He turned to look at the marshal. 'With Moran out of the way, and me downed, the way's clear.'

'You figure tonight?'

'Well, pretty soon they'll know from Blane I got up

off the floor. But a slug in the shoulder's slowed me down, and if Waggoner's already fired up and rarin' to go. . . .'

'Yeah,' Sam Sloan said, grimacing. 'With four gunnies and Blane's dozen cowhands, they've got a small army.'

'Way too much for us to handle,' Cleet said, and he deliberately made his gaze neutral as he met the marshal's eyes.

And now Sloan smiled happily. 'Except I listened to camp-fire tales about a deadly gunslinger called J.C. Cleet for more years than I can count,' he said. 'If one tenth of what I've heard is true – and most of what I read in those papers on my desk is lies – then I've got a good man alongside me who could win this little range war on his own – and that's with one arm.'

Chapter Nine

What benefit does a man get from talking – or being talked to?

If Cleet had asked himself that question as he rode into Old Town after the long ride down the Bravo from Eagle Pass he would have been lost for an answer, and the question itself would have become irrelevant once his gaze was drawn towards the rays of the setting sun falling on the façade of the New Deal saloon.

But if for so long the next border town and the next reeking saloon had been the height of his ambitions then, in forty-eight hours, brief brushes with violence and tragedy and a few words from two very different people – and what amounted to a declaration of trust – had caused some deep soul-searching. The shiny deputy's badge pinned to his bloodstained shirt told him that a decent, small-town lawman had disregarded an unsavoury reputation and accepted him at face value; the look in the eyes of a young girl whose marriage had been falling apart when she lost her husband sent Cleet to the cracked piece of mirror in the shabby rooming-house, and the sight he saw there – hell, he thought, the sight he'd looked at in every saloon bar mirror in Texas but never truly seen – took him from the mirror to the wash bowl on the stand in his room and saw him snapping open his little-used cut-throat razor.

That act itself – awkward as it was with his injured shoulder – was enough to send his thoughts chasing down his back-trail and, as always, the old bitterness rose like bile in his throat. He had never knowingly killed a man other than in self defence, yet tales told in the flickering light of a hundred camp-fires had embellished the truth so that each time he was involved in gunplay the reputation spread by word of mouth counted against him. The men he downed when he had permitted them to draw first were sinned against, lawmen got wind of his name and the price on his head was hiked accordingly.

And so it had gone on, would almost certainly have gone on to this day, had it not been for young Simon Van Haan and the coloured chips that were scattered across the card-table as he fell dead in the sawdust of a San Angelo saloon . . .

The ache in his shoulder and the pain of scraping off week-old stubble broke into Cleet's bitter thoughts and he became aware of faint voices from the square that drew him to the open window. Sam Sloan was leaning against the hitch rail in front of the jail talking to Chrissy Moran. The afternoon sun glinted on his badge and touched the girl's dark hair with gold. There was grace in her stance, and with it an allure that stirred Cleet's senses from clear across the breadth of the square and saw him unconsciously straighten his back and square his shoulder.

As he did so, awareness of what he was thinking hit him hard. He touched the lather on his face with a sheepish grin and, considerably abashed, completed his ablutions with the soft sound of the girl's tinkling laughter seeming to emphasize his foolishness.

Nevertheless, with his face clean and shiny, greying hair brushed slick and a clean if crumpled shirt tucked into his pants, Cleet was impressed enough with his appearance to walk out of the room with something close to a swagger. His mortification had receded gradually as he shaved, some hard thinking had reminded him of a duty he had failed to perform and, as he clattered down the stairs with his mind on Old Town's blacksmith and what he wanted the man to do, Cleet was mentally willing Chrissy to wait around for a while longer.

'I don't know if I'm ready for this,' she said.

'It's a plot of ground where a man's at peace,' Cleet said. 'Think of it that way, let me do the rest.'

She was tense in the saddle, her nostrils already flaring as they rode into the harsh stink of the still smouldering ashes and she looked across the ruins of her home to the solid wall of dark trees.

'I think I should stay back out of the way.'

87

'No.' He shook his head, smiled reassuringly. 'There's something I want you to see.'

Fine grey ash spurted from beneath the horses' hooves as they skirted the ruins and crossed the small clearing. The sun was low in the west, the shadows swiftly lengthening and, despite the heat of the day, it was already cool in the deeper shade at the edge of the woods. Chill, Cleet thought, the chill of death – and even as the thought struck him he saw Chrissy shiver.

Then he was out of the saddle. From his saddle-bag he took a length of thin rawhide and a flat object wrapped in sacking, turned away from her and went to the dark mound of fresh earth. He had dug up enough rocks when burying Pete Moran, and now he snapped off a thick branch and used one of the heavier rocks to drive it into the ground at the head of the grave. Then he unwrapped the sacking and took out the flat head-board with the words burnt into it by Old Town's blacksmith and, still with his back to the girl, used the rawhide thong to lash it to the upright.

Straightening, he stepped back, and to one side.

'Pete Moran,' she read softly. 'R.I.P.'

'There should be more,' he said, 'but I guess I'm not too good with words.'

'It's beautiful.'

She slid from the saddle and walked over to him, reached up to take his face in both her hands, and kissed him gently on the lips. Still holding his face she pulled back and looked up into his eyes.

'Thank you, J.C. Cleet.'

'My pleasure, ma'am.'

He had taken her hand softly in his and they were standing in silence at the foot of the grave when the distant rattle of hooves came to them. The sound rose and fell, then swelled to a deep, insistent drumming, and long shadows chased across the ground as a bunch of riders came hammering down the banks of the Bravo.

And it was with a feeling of reluctance laced with inevitablility – for he was, after all, wearing a deputy's badge – that Cleet again returned to his saddle-bag. This time what he took out was not a humble memorial to one man's short life, but shiny instruments of death: he unwrapped the bone-handled six-guns, buckled the belt around his waist and with an act of finality tied the cords securing the holsters around his lean thighs.

Chapter Ten

The flickering oil lamp cast a smoky light over the table in the jail's cell-room. It threw the eyes of the two men sitting there into deep shadow, emphasized the hollows beneath cheekbones and gave to their faces a sinister aspect that was heightened by the tightness of their jaws and the tension in the room that was like the silent calm before the eruption of a violent electrical storm.

Forearms resting on the table as he absently rubbed one of his six-guns with an oily rag, Judson Cleet said, 'I guess there's no chance of raising a posse – if we need one?'

Sloan smiled bleakly. 'The men willing to ride are so old it'd take both of us to boost them into the saddle. Those able to ride and fight left Old Town when they were in short pants, spend most of their time raisin' hell in Laredo or San Anton'.'

'So it's up to that feller you heard about around camp-fires.'

'I reckon.'

'You know he doesn't exist – and never did?'

'Sure.'

Cleet lifted the pistol and squinted into the barrel. 'And you're prepared to risk riding with the man who's a thin shadow of that reputation?'

'I'm interested in what a man intends to do, not what he's done.'

Cleet put down the pistol, and nodded thoughtfully. 'What's your gut feeling, Sloan?'

'Rivera'll come out on top.'

'Mex *vaqueros*, in a shootout against gunslingers of Johnny Van Haan's calibre?'

'All down to numbers. If I know Don Diego, he'll be at the head of his men and ride straight over those Texans.'

'Won't Waggoner have calculated for that?'

'And?'

'Come up with a better idea.'

'Like what?'

'I don't know.' Cleet poked a finger into the pistol's trigger guard, watched it absently as he moved it in a slow circle on the desk's scarred surface. 'But he needs something to tip the scales his way.'

'Look,' Sloan said, 'you saw a bunch of riders heading down the Bravo?'

'Right.'

'Four or five – or a dozen or more?'

'I picked out Van Haan and the Mex. Blane was there, and most of his crew.' Cleet looked up. 'Fourteen ⸻een, I'd say.'

'And did they look like they had fancy ideas?'

Cleet smiled wryly. 'What the hell does that mean?'

'Exactly.' Sloan stood up, started towards the office, then stopped. 'Fifteen men with six-guns and rifles, looking for a fight. A couple of miles down the line they'd have crossed the river, headed west. Bunched up, they'll sound like the 7th Cavalry on the move. Don Diego will be ready for them, and I'd put the odds in his favour at three to one. If Waggoner and Blane have got sense—'

'I didn't see Waggoner,' Cleet said, eyes narrowed.

'D'you think that's important? I can't see it – and anyway, who cares? If Blane's in charge, and has got the sense God gave him, he'll take a look at the odds and turn back. If he doesn't . . ..' Sloan shook his head and again turned away. 'Slipping across the Bravo to steal a couple of stray steers is one thing, but setting out to steal a *ranchero*'s entire stock. . . .'

His voice trailed off as he went into the office. A coffee pot clanged on iron. Tin rattled. Liquid gurgled. When he returned, Sloan was holding two steaming cups. He set them on the table, sat down, lifted an eyebrow at Cleet.

'Now what?'

Cleet took a breath, let it out slowly. 'You talk a good fight, Sloan, and I can't fault your line of thought. But it occurred to me that if you've always been convinced Rivera will come out on top, why the hell did you give me a badge?'

'Didn't I tell you it was that or throw you in a cell?'

'Sure you did – but why offer me a way out?'

Sloan sipped his coffee and thought for a while, and when he looked at Cleet again his blue eyes were mildly amused.

'Maybe that reveals something about the both of us that was buried deep and fighting to get out. Yesterday you asked me why the change of heart? One minute you were free to go, the next I was forcing you to stay on my terms. Hell, I even surprised myself. The infamous J.C. Cleet walks into my jail, ends up flat on his back in a cell and it's plumb certain that if I dig through those dodgers there's a reward there for the taking.'

'So why?'

'Christ, man, you're still young—'

'Pushing fifty—'

'—and I saw something in your eyes, and despite what I saw there – a contradiction; it told me there was a good, honest man inside the body of a derelict – I knew that if you walked out of here there'd be—'

'Another town. Another bar.' Cleet picked up his cup, tasted the strong, hot java, felt the sudden urge for something with more kick and was at once astounded by how easily it was quelled. Sloan was right, of course: for more years than Cleet cared to remember it had always been the next town, the next glass of cheap whiskey. And Sloan was right, too, in that what he had said revealed something in the small-town lawman's character that had, perhaps, come as a surprise. Hell, he'd admitted as much.

But was he mistaken? Sam Sloan was as fallible as the next man, and years spent lazing in the Texas sun while the town around him died a slow death could distort a man's thinking, turn dreams into longings and cause the sheen of strong drink in a pair of tired grey eyes to look like the inner fire that had for so long been missing from his own.

That was the downside. And wrong. Old Town's somnolence had touched the marshal, yes, but it seemed that Cleet's coming had lifted him from incipient torpor and given him a purpose. And, at this conclusion, Cleet was forced to suppress a grin. His thinking had brought him full circle. Two men with a renewed purpose in life had taken to philosophizing and ended up close to slapping each other on the back, and Cleet had already opened his mouth to point this out when he realized the marshal was no longer with him.

Sam Sloan had turned away and, as the look on the marshal's face hit him, Cleet caught the faint sounds of an approaching horse. It came on steadily, not being pushed hard, yet in that inexorable approach there was a foreboding that brought Judson Cleet up out of his chair and sent Sam Sloan running for the door.

Chapter Eleven

'You are certain?

There was sympathy in the old Mexican's watery eyes as he considered how to answer the question. 'Her horse is not in the corral. And you yourself have not seen her since late morning, when Sloan and the other man were here with more wasted words.' He shrugged, and when he shook his head his face was graven by an inner sorrow.

Don Diego Rivera had half turned to gaze across the yard towards the westering sun. Evening was approaching and the warm light softened his face, but his hands were clasped in front of him and the knuckles showed white.

'But if she was thrown from her horse,' he said, 'and managed to cling to the reins. . . .'

'There is that possibility,' said the old man.

'A possibility.' Rivera nodded. 'But not a probability?'

'Not even a likelihood,' said the old man.

'And if I organize a search – as I must – it will mean leaving the herds unprotected, while those Texans. . . .'

Again his voice trailed, and now he turned to the old man, Octavio, who had been an employee and a trusted friend of the Rivera family for more than sixty years, and said softly, 'If my wife was alive she would know what to do.'

'If your wife was alive,' said Octavio with a toothless grimace, 'she would tell you what to do – and you would do it.'

'But now,' Don Diego said, feigning deeply wounded pride, 'I must rely on a man who has much of her wisdom, but none of her tact.' Then his eyes softened, and he reached out to touch the old man's arm. 'My daughter is missing, my herds are penned but by no means safe – tell me, Octavio, my old friend, what am I to do?'

The answer was not what he expected.

'You must consider carefully the dust cloud to the east,' said Octavio. 'I noticed it a short while ago. Even as we spoke and your eyes were drawn to the west, I looked the other way and wondered – perhaps hoped a little. But I know now it is not the dust kicked up by a single rider returning home: it is the men you feared, the Texan renegades who are after the beef of Don Diego—'

'Alert the men!'

With a swift glance, Rivera had taken in the high, drifting plume of dust, tried futilely to penetrate the still distant veil and identify the riders kicking up the storm and, with a final look at the low ridge over which the riders would eventually approach the ranch, had swung lithely away. Still trim, still light on his feet despite advancing age and with the thoughts that had dwelt morbidly on the possible fate of his missing daughter now brought slamming back to earth by the threat of danger, he was jogging towards the house even as the old retainer's surprisingly firm voice rang out across the yard.

In Don Diego's mind as he ran there was not panic, but a smouldering anger that was born of frustration and an admission of his own lack of preparation. After all, he reminded himself bitterly, he had for many months been awaiting the arrival of the renegade Texans. If the common sense displayed by Octavio and attributed to his late wife had been matched by his own, he would have done more than talk of this and that to Sam Sloan and, over cups of potent mescal drunk around flickering camp-fires, tell his grinning *vaqueros* to prepare for the worst.

As he slammed into the house, plucked a gleaming Winchester rifle from the rack and plunged back towards the late sunlight splashing through the door, Rivera was already aware of the swelling tumult outside. He burst through the door to see men running. They were shouting as they ran from the bunkhouse and the corrals, from barns and kitchens, some with raven hair tousled and rubbing sleep from their eyes, others caked in dust and bearing the stink of cattle on their dark skins, still others reddened by the heat of the stoves and with dark sweat staining their under-shirts. But all carried guns – for had he not warned them never to be without – and even as their dark, flashing eyes flew to the old retainer who was an imperious figure in the centre of the yard, they were casting excited glances to the east and the thin dust cloud that was now a storm fast approaching.

'Enough!' Don Diego Rivera roared. 'Calm down, all of you. Stand still, just where you are – and listen.'

The shouting ceased. Like children in a schoolyard they stopped and stood, feet shuffling, a wild variety of pistols and rifles glittering wickedly in the sunshine as they faced Rivera. But these, he thought proudly, were not children. They were mature working men, strong, armed, and plenty of them; more than enough, surely, to take care of a handful of Texan shootists? How many had Pete Moran mentioned? Six, at the very most – and hadn't the gunman, Cleet, eliminated two of those with his deadly skill? Just one lightning swift calculation as his eyes ranged the yard, told Rivera that he could already count on more than fifteen, and there were laggards still to come. And as he took a deep breath and lifted himself so that he was as they must always perceive Don Diego Rivera, he saw a powerful man – his foreman, Ramon – move to the fore carrying a Sharps buffalo gun, and drew from his strength.

'Listen to me,' he said, choosing his words with care. 'The men we have expected are coming now – but they are not coming in the manner I expected.' He cleared his throat, looked at the sea of dark, attentive eyes. 'I would have expected them to come in darkness, to sweep down on you as most of you slept. Instead, they are riding here in daylight. That has obvious benefits, but it also creates problems: we do not know *why* they are doing this.'

Rivera paused, let the men absorb the words and chew on their meaning; saw several men nod understanding, others whisper to those still puzzled.

'And so,' he continued, 'we must move quickly to be ready – and then we must wait.'

Enough words.

He summoned his foreman, gave terse instructions, then moved back to stand in front of the house with the aged Octavio as the *vaqueros* were despatched to their positions. The yard emptied. Nimble figures carrying pistols and rifles scurried behind barns and bunkhouse, behind the house itself – even, Rivera noticed with a fleeting gleam of amusement in his dark eyes, behind the cluster of mighty saguaros standing on the arid mound to the north.

In a few short minutes, Don Diego was left alone with Octavio, and the foreman, Ramon. A thin dust was settling. To the perceptive observer there would be the sense and scent of humanity, of sweat and gun-oil, and over all the crackle of tension, for those tense few minutes of preparation had been barely enough. The last man was still slipping behind cover with the clink of a rifle barrel on stone and a flash of white cloth when Ramon swore softly as the first riders appeared over the gentle rise some 500 yards to the east – and halted.

Alongside Rivera, the old retainer's lips moved as

his gnarled hands made the sign of the cross.

More than sixteen of them, Rivera judged, eyes narrowed as he squinted across the distance. But of course, he thought, with considerable disgust. It was their intention to drive away his cattle. How could he have imagined that, with just four men. . . .

He looked at Octavio, and what he saw in the old man's eyes caused him to shiver. I have never seen my old friend afraid, Rivera thought. But now the fear is naked in his eyes, yet it is not for himself—

'Two men riding in,' the foreman, Ramon, said in a growling, basso voice. 'The rest they leave behind.'

'They bring an ultimatum,' said Octavio, and suddenly the firm tones that had rung loud and clear across the yard were ineffably weary.

'Let them come,' said Rivera. 'Ramon, keep hold of your rifle but do not be aggressive.'

It took an age for the two riders to draw near, for Rivera to be able to step away from the shadow of the house where he had moved to rest his rifle against the wall and say bitterly to his compadres, 'I know them, from the dead young Ranger's description. The Texan is Van Haan. The other, the Mexican, is a man called Diaz.'

'Killers,' said Ramon.

'Then let us pray,' said Octavio.

And then the two riders were pushing up the slope into the yard, their horses' hooves clopping on the packed earth, the lean man in dusty black clothing moving ahead with a Winchester held easily across his thighs. Above a lean, stubbled face his pale eyes were chillingly reflective in the light of the fading sun.

'Rivera?'

The lathered horse halted and tossed its head, bit jingling.

'*Sí*. What is it you want here with your men and your pistols, and your bravado?'

Behind the black-clad rider, the scarred Mexican with the milk-white eye wheeled his horse to a halt and laughed.

'Not what I want, old man,' said the man in black. 'It's what you want.'

'All right,' Rivera said. 'Amuse me before you leave. Tell me what I want.'

'You want your daughter back,' the black-clad gunman said, and Octavio, the retainer, moaned softly.

'You have her?' Rivera's voice was tight, his gaze instinctively flashing to the distant group of horsemen.

'Not here. Nor anywhere near.'

'Then where?'

'First, I'll tell you what we want—'

'With respect, I already know what you want.'

'Then the talking's all done so—'

'No!'

At Rivera's sudden sharp cry a black bird rose heavily from the roof of the house and flapped away towards the blood-red glare of the sinking sun.

'No,' Rivera said more quietly, his voice husky but lined with steel. 'The talking is not over because your men are over there and you are here, and we have not yet established the facts.'

The Mexican, Diaz, spat wetly. '*Madre de Dios*, will you listen to the man, Haan? We got his daughter, and all he wants is to talk tough.'

To Rivera, Van Haan said, 'Are you telling me we're in trouble? From a bunch of Mex *peon*?'

'If I lift my hand,' Rivera said, 'you will both die from a dozen gunshot wounds. If my daughter is not here, nor anywhere near here, why should I not do that?'

'Jesus!' Van Haan said. 'Stop wasting time. Your daughter's in Texas with a couple of men frettin' and fumin' until they see a herd of cows comin' across the Bravo. Your cows. Sooner that happens, sooner your worries are over.'

Suddenly, Rivera felt numb. It was as if the fight had gone from him, simply trickled away like fine dry sand. He could see clearly, and understand the situation – but his mind refused to look at any solution other than the obvious.

Thickly, he said, 'I get her back? Safe? Unharmed? If I . . . if I give these men what they want?'

'In time.'

'But now is time. I do it now.' He shook his head. 'I do not understand.'

'Safe passage.' Van Haan grinned. 'If your daughter gets us the herd, she also guarantees my friends keep hold of it – all the way up the Chisholm to Kansas.'

Chapter Twelve

'They also demanded a bill of sale,' Don Diego Rivera said, 'using the same threat to coerce' – he grinned savagely – 'to force me into acquiescence.'

Despite the sweat on his face and the trail dust powdering his dark clothing, his language and demeanour were almost haughty as he stood stiffly just inside Sam Sloan's office with the big *vaquero*, Ramon, at his shoulder. No, imperious was a better description, Cleet decided. *That's what he has to be: he's told us he's been robbed, his pride's been hurt bad by gringo bandits, and rising above it is the only way he knows. And now he's facing a couple more* gringos . . .

'So Blane's about to push your herd up the Bravo, using a remuda he bought from you with hard cash?' Sloan looked at Rivera for confirmation, saw his nod, and went on. 'He's also got a bill of sale telling the world he's the legal owner of that herd – and Lupe Waggoner's holding your daughter, Maria, as insurance – against what?'

'I let them go. No challenge. No law.'

'How far?'

'To the Red, maybe. Then she is free.'

'And you'll go along with that?'

Rivera shrugged. 'It is . . . what do they call it? An impasse?'

'Stand-off paints a better picture,' Cleet said.

'And is that what we do?'

The air drifting through the door was still clogged with the smell of sun-baked dust, though the street was dark and oil lamps glimmered in the windows of the café and the livery barn across the square. At the hitch rail outside the jail, the two Mexicans' horses steamed gently as they dozed in the cooling night air. A door flapped open across the way. Light flooded out and Cleet heard a woman's voice, soft and low, as soothing as a cool hand on a damp brow when a man is all fired up with anger.

'You tell me, Don Diego,' Sam Sloan said. He reached out to touch a half-empty bottle of whiskey and look questioningly at the Mexican, pushed it to one side at the man's quick shake of the head, then scratched a match on a scarred area of desk and let it flare in his cupped hand as he looked at the *ranchero*. 'Standin' off gets us nowhere, chasing after them's a matter of climbin' on a horse – but then I can see the situation some miles up the line where we're forced to stop and pull back when they hold a pistol to your daughter's head.'

'But it is your job to extricate yourself from difficult situations,' Rivera said as Sloan applied the flame to

106

the bowl of his pipe, puffed a cloud of smoke. He moved away from the door, scraped a chair across the floor, straddled it restlessly. 'You are a lawman, Sam Sloan. I am a Mexican businessman reporting a crime committed by your countrymen. Do you intend doing anything, or nothing?'

In the doorway, the big *vaquero*, Ramon, said scathingly, 'Better we had done the job ourselves, we know the land that side of the river—'

'They moving them up the west bank? Stayin' on the Mexican side?' Suddenly alert, Sloan held the smoking pipe poised as he looked from the *vaquero* to Rivera. 'That's not what I figured.'

Ramon snorted his disgust and stepped out into the night.

'They cannot cross safely until daylight,' Rivera said patiently, 'so they make up some ground first. That way, when they do take the herd across the river at sun-up they will be in a position to head due east towards San Antonio and the cattle trail north.'

'So we take them at the river, hit them as they cross?' Sloan cocked an eyebrow at Cleet.

Cleet nodded. 'Makes sense to do that. At that time they'll be blinded by the sun. We catch them right they'll be up past their saddles in muddy water, pistols likely to misfire, panicked longhorns climbing up their backs to get out the river. With rifles, the sun at our backs, we could pick them off from a distance.'

'But how do we avoid the problem caused by the girl?'

'Go for Waggoner, or Blane. With them out of the way the rest'll have no stomach for a fight.'

Sloan sucked his pipe, nodding slowly, then caught the slow shake of Rivera's head.

'Waggoner and Blane are not with the herd,' said the *ranchero*.

Cleet swore softly. 'Sure they're not! Diaz and Van Haan and the 'punchers Blane brought in are moving the cattle. Blane and Waggoner will be holding Maria at the camp upriver.'

'But if that's so,' Sloan said, 'and Van Haan and Diaz can't bring the herd across until sun-up—'

'Don Diego,' Cleet cut in, 'how many Texans came calling on you?'

The *ranchero* pursed his lips. 'Fifteen or sixteen. . . .' He shrugged.

'The whole bunch,' Cleet said, 'leaving Waggoner and Blane—'

He broke off and looked towards the door as Chrissy Moran came in. She was trim in denim pants and shirt, a serge jacket keeping out the chill, a flat black hat on dark hair brushed to a lustrous sheen. Ramon was a massive shape looming behind her, and Cleet smiled inwardly as the man's black eyes caught the glint of lamplight. Put a pretty girl in front of a man. . . .

Chrissy was looking at Rivera, concern in her dark eyes.

'I can think of only one reason why you'd be in Old Town at this time of night, Don Diego.'

The Mexican had risen from the chair, and now he dipped his head.

'It is as your husband predicted, *señora*. The Texans have crossed the river, and taken my herds.'

'I'm sure your men fought hard.'

'Not a single shot was fired.'

'But—'

'They'd already taken his daughter,' Sloan said through a curl of smoke. 'There was nothing he could do.'

'But can't *we* do something? Anything? Are we going to let them get away with it?' This was to Cleet, not Sloan, and he nodded quickly, his mind alive with crazy thoughts. *Put a pretty girl in front of a man.* And what was it this young woman had said? *I carried a pistol, rode alongside Pete.* She'd had the guts to do that and now, given the chance, she'd be keen to get back at the men who'd burned her home, hanged her husband. Hell, she was pretty enough to bring a saint down the wrong side of the fence and, handled right, the risks would be small.

Still nodding, Cleet saw Sam Sloan watching him keenly and knew the marshal had seen the sudden light in his eyes.

Slowly, still thinking ahead, Cleet said, 'Chrissy, are you up to a night ride?'

'Sure, if it'll help – but to where?'

But now Sam Sloan was following Cleet's train of thought, and as the marshal's sharp mind cottoned on to the possibilities he tapped his teeth pensively with the stem of his pipe. 'I guess,' he said, 'what Cleet's sayin' is we need something eye catching to grab those fellers' attention for a short spell.'

Chrissy stared, then laughed. 'And you'd trust me to do that?'

'You're a grief-stricken young woman,' Cleet said, thinking it through. 'You find it impossible to sleep, something drags you back to the ruins of your home, next thing you know you're riding north along the Bravo and stumble into an encampment. You're not thinking straight. Maybe there's some tears. The fellers there can't get any sense out of you . . . can't take their eyes off you—'

'Catch them with their pants down,' Chrissy said, her face animated. 'You're right, and I'm sure I can do it. I was listening outside, with Ramon. They're on their own up there, just the two of them with Maria. If I ride in, get their minds fixed on something other than their pistols. . . .'

She let the words trail away and Cleet knew she'd suddenly seen the harsh, shocking image and had begun living the terror of a young woman riding in out of the night to a crackling camp-fire on the banks of the Bravo where flickering flames cast an eerie light on gleaming pistols and the faces of two men, evil men, rustlers who were already callously using a young woman . . . and, in the background, the pale face and wide dark eyes of that frightened young woman.

'Your husband is no longer with us,' Diego Rivera said softly. 'You rode with him, yes, but I cannot ask

110

you to risk your life—'

'We'll be with her all the way,' Sloan said, and there was finality in his actions as he tapped the smouldering dottle from his pipe and stowed it in his pocket. 'We'll ride in ahead of her, take up positions close enough to move in fast if we're needed. They'll hear her coming, figure there's just one rider – see her when she rides into the circle of light, know she's unarmed, a pretty slip of a girl.'

'And then?' Still out of his chair, pacing now, Rivera was frowning. He stopped close to Chrissy and touched her arm, shook his head and moved alongside the big *vaquero*. 'No! In my heart I know it is wrong. Ramon should ride with you. This brave young woman must not risk her life, the three of you together would surely be able—'

'That'd be fine,' Sam Sloan said, coming around the desk to take his gunbelt down from its wall peg, 'if you're daughter wasn't involved,' and Cleet saw the elegant Mexican's shoulders droop. Feller's realized his mistake, he thought. Poor man's clutching at straws, wants his daughter back but he's all torn apart by the thought of another young woman getting involved. But that young woman wants to be part of this, he's going to have to accept—

'While you're at it,' Chrissy Moran said, as Sloan buckled on his gunbelt, 'dig me out a pistol, one I can put in my belt round back under my jacket. If something clicks with those two meatheads and they start getting ugly—'

111

Rivera sighed softly, a low exhalation of distress. 'You have those thoughts, – yet still you are going through with this?'

'Over-active imagination, Don Diego,' Chrissy said, flashing a grin. 'If I paid heed to that I'd never get out of bed.'

'Then my duty is clear: it is I who must ride with you.'

'No.' Sloan shook his head. He settled his holster, gave it a final slap and turned away from the *ranchero*'s look of disbelief.

'You have a good reason why I should not?'

As Sloan stamped towards the door, it was Cleet gave the answer. 'If the bullets start flying out there in the woods and that young woman's caught in the middle, the last person we want alongside us is her father.'

'But I give you my word—'

'Don't. Because whatever you believe now, if what I just suggested comes about, you won't keep it.'

'I am a gentleman—'

'Sure, but first, you're a father.'

'But—'

And then, as Cleet looked into his eyes, unblinking, willing to stand there all night if need be, the *ranchero* wilted. Maybe, Cleet thought, as his own taut muscles relaxed, his imagination was as active as Chrissy Moran's and his mind had taken him to a dark place of unimaginable horror where blood matted lustrous dark hair and a young woman screamed. Or maybe he'd seen something in Cleet's eyes that would not have been there when the former shootist rode into Old Town in search of the next saloon, the next drink. Cleet liked to believe it was that, and was half convinced that the answer he sought was etched on the elderly Mexican's countenance as he sighed, and shrugged.

'Then, if your mind is made up and you must go without me,' Rivera said, '*vaya con Dios*,' and there was a catch in his voice and his dark eyes were liquid with emotion. 'Go with God, every one of you – and, God willing, return safely with my daughter.'

Part Two
Cleet Rides Out

Chapter Thirteen

Court Blane's sweating 'punchers moved the last of
Diego Rivera's bawling, protesting steers out of the
vast pens at Buena Vista by full dark. By midnight, the
herd was strung out in a three-mile line like a thick-
bodied arrow pointing north-east across the grassland
towards the Bravo, a big, scarred steer had stamped its
authority over lesser animals and moved to the head of
the column, and the two point riders were dozing in the
saddle as they anticipated the river crossing that lay
some way and some hours ahead.

Diaz and Van Haan were half a mile behind the
'punchers riding swing, but well out on the eastern
flank to avoid the pall of dust that was drifting high
and long to mask the high stars' brilliance and settle in
choking clouds over the stoical drag riders. Much
earlier – before the move from Buena Vista – Concho
and the kid had broken into an old adobe shed and
discovered Rivera's stock of wine in the mouldering
gloom, and the last Johnny Van Haan had seen of them

they were sprawled on the ground outside with their backs to the wall, several empty bottles scattered around them and the kid's battered harmonica wailing.

Once, after some hours' riding, he twisted in the saddle to look back, and Diaz grinned ferociously.

'Most likely some old woman has hobbled out of the kitchen and used her carving knife to slit their throats,' he said, and spat drily towards Van Haan.

'We don't need them,' Van Haan said. 'After the girl was taken, nary a one of us was needed. Rivera's hands are tied so tight all he can do is kiss his steers goodbye and start prayin'.'

'I don' know,' Diaz said. His eye gleamed white as he looked sideways at Van Haan. ' Maybe Rivera say one thing, mean another. You see when we ride in to Buena Vista, how those *vaqueros* with their pistols and rifles vanish like jack-rabbits? There, then not there. But not scared, I think. What I think is, they are out there now, seeing but not seen.'

A match flared in the darkness, lighting the hard planes of Van Haan's face as he applied the flame to his cigarette.

'We'll know for sure,' he said, 'when the slug you don't hear takes you in the back and knocks you clean out of the saddle.'

'*Gracias, amigo,*' Diaz with heavy sarcasm, 'but I think maybe you are wrong, they take the gringo first and then I ride away from this whole, crazy business.'

'Maybe we'll both ride away,' Van Haan said, then swore under his breath and heaved on the reins as a rider ripped by out of the darkness, kicking up dust and using his pony's skill and the end of a short, swinging rope to bring a frisky steer loping back towards the main column.

'And right now seems like a good time to do it,' he finished as the dust settled, and with a decisive flick he sent the half-smoked cigarette sparking into the darkness.

'You think?'

'Concho and the kid are out of it. If those *vaqueros* are trackin' us, and move in for the kill, there ain't nothing we can do.'

'Is true,' Diaz said, and saddle leather creaked as he swung away from the rumble of the herd. 'Me, I think it is time we cross the river and discuss with Waggoner the *dinero* given to him by Court Blane – before it is too late.'

'Amen to that,' said Van Haan.

'How's the shoulder?'

'Itching like crazy.'

'That's good!' Chrissy looked behind as if demanding confirmation and, ten yards back down the trail, Sam Sloan laughed.

'Try telling him that when he's using his left hand to hold a rifle steady.'

'Only way that can happen tonight,' Cleet said, 'is if we can see them by the light of the camp-fire – always supposing they've kept it alight.'

'Likely they have,' Sloan said, spurring closer. 'That

girl's got Rivera's spirit. They don't keep their eye on her she'll slip away into the woods, nail both of 'em with a rock if they're fools enough to give chase.'

'Lord, I hope she does that and makes it all the way home,' Chrissy Moran said fervently. 'Don Diego and his *vaqueros* will be after those renegade Texans like a horde of avenging angels.'

'Instead of which,' Sloan said, 'he's settin' back there in Old Town wondering why the hell he ain't allowed to go chasin' after his own daughter.'

'Hah!' Chrissy said scornfully. 'You think that? Before I walked into your office I was talking to Ramon. He didn't say much, but the gist of it was that if anybody's going to get Maria away from Waggoner, it'll be him and Don Diego.' She chuckled. 'He said he wouldn't trust you to take eggs from under a chicken without breaking them.'

'Ramon ain't Don Diego,' Sloan said easily, 'and I reckon my new deputy spelled things out pretty clear for the old feller.' With a click of his tongue he put spurs to his horse and pulled past Chrissy and Cleet.

They rode in silence for the next half-hour, cutting hard across country towards the Bravo then swinging north when the clear, starlit skies revealed the gleam of the river and their horses' ears pricked at the rank smell of its waters. A short while after that they passed the still smouldering heap of charred timber that had been Chrissy Moran's home, and for some way the silence was filled with dark thoughts that strengthened resolve. From there, they knew, the Waggoner encampment was but a few miles upriver and, as they pushed on through the night, it was as if the air was suddenly crackling with tension.

For Cleet, as he rode, that tension assaulted him from two directions: he was thinking ahead, of what was to come, but at the same time the Old Town marshal's words lingered with him. Sure he'd made it clear to Don Diego that, as a father inflamed by the thought of his daughter's peril, if he came after Waggoner he'd likely lose control, cut loose and get in the way – yet still Cleet found himself facing front but half listening for sounds from down their back-trail.

The suspicion that Rivera and the big *vaquero* might be slipping silently through the night somewhere behind them was further intensified when he recalled the look in the *ranchero*'s eyes as he gave the lawmen and the girl his blessing. What had it revealed? Had he read it right? Emotion was there, no doubt of that, but how should it be interpreted? Cleet had taken it for deep concern for his daughter and a burning desire to see the two lawmen succeed, the Moran girl come through safely. But now he realized it could just as easily have been a fierce determination to hunt down Waggoner himself and personally rescue his daughter.

But if so, why ride into Old Town to see Sam Sloan?

Well, Cleet thought with some amusement, maybe, after all, he wasn't giving the old *ranchero* the credit he deserved. Maybe Rivera was shrewd enough to realize he and Ramon could do with some help, so why not talk to Sam Sloan, let him and that deadly shootist Judson Cleet do the hard work, but be on hand to take some of the credit?

Or maybe, Cleet thought irritably, the monotonous pounding of hooves was getting to him and he'd imagined himself into a mental box canyon because reports of a big *vaquero*'s bravado in front of a pretty girl had led him to misinterpret the look in a tired old man's eyes.

Don Diego was back in Old Town, his feet on Sam Sloan's desk, a glass of the marshal's rot-gut whiskey in his elegant hand. Ramon? Hell, Ramon was probably doing the same in the New Deal while the big, black-eyed barman yawned cavernously, cursed him silently and thought longingly of his bed.

'I wonder,' Don Diego Rivera said carefully, 'if we should perhaps be going about this in a different way?'

'You are beginning to sound like that timid old woman, Octavio,' Ramon said with undisguised scorn. 'There is always another way, but in most cases there is just the one *right* way.'

'Ah, yes,' said Rivera, the metal bit tinkling as he turned in the saddle, 'but it takes a clever man to know which is which, and great care must be taken when there are lives at stake.'

'One life! Maria's. The others are not our concern.'

'Ramon, my friend, you have the heart of a lion, the sentiments of a rattlesnake—'

'And enough God-given intelligence to understand

that actions speak louder than words. All those gringo bastards holding Maria can hear is the music of gold eagles jingling at the end of the long trail north.' The big *vaquero* grinned, and slapped the big Sharps .50 lying across his massive thighs. 'With this, I will play them a different, deadlier tune.'

To Rivera, the deceptively casual talk as they rode through the darkness was akin to thinking out loud, something he and Ramon often did when they were together. It was an instinctive habit born of years of familiarity, and while both men had been trading ideas and insults, their ears had been carefully tuned to the sounds of night. Each was aware that Sloan, Cleet and the girl were no more than half a mile ahead, and their ears were sharp enough to pick up the occasional faint clink of hooves carried on the still air, the jingle of bridles, the sharp snap of a twig.

But Rivera was deeply concerned. Pride had made him loth to leave the rescue of Maria to his friend, the Old Town marshal, but half an hour of thinking out loud with the admirable Ramon had suggested no right way or wrong way to go about it. By taking his daughter, Waggoner *had* created an impasse – or stand-off, Rivera corrected, grinning without humour in the darkness. And the maverick Texan had a partner. Even by the light of a flickering camp-fire Ramon, with his Sharps breechloader, was skilful enough to bring down one man but, in the time taken for the *vaquero* to reload, the second man would be out of his blankets and have his pistol to the girl's head.

So it was a matter of wait and see, thought Rivera; of simply being true to character – and this time his smile was one of genuine amusement, for what was seen by *gringos* to be the laziness of all Mexicans was, more often than they could be expected to understand, an eternal patience that brought its own rich rewards.

And, *por favor*, he thought fervently, let me tonight have the patience to ensure that those rewards do not melt away into the darkness and leave me clutching nothing but memories, and sadness.

Chapter Fourteen

They smelt the fire with a suddenness that was shocking, its urgent pungency cutting through the damp mist drifting off the Rio Bravo to their left and the smoke, once identified, hanging visibly like flat skeins of dew-kissed gossamer in the branches where the brightening moonlight ahead of them touched the trees. Using their night vision they looked out of the sides of their eyes, squinting into the confusing, dappled shade and at last picking out the faintest of yellow flickers.

No more than 200 yards ahead. To the right of the wide trail that followed the river-bank. The land flat, but with a useful rise beyond the trees away from the river. And now, between the trees and the rise, Cleet picked out a corral rigged from lass-ropes, the vague shapes of a number of horses: Court Blane's remuda.

'Almost rode straight over them,' Cleet warned, pulling off the hard ground into the coarse, damp grass and waiting for the others to draw alongside.

'Time for you and me to make ourselves scarce,' said Sam Sloan, and Cleet saw Chrissy shiver.

'They'll expect a show of nerves,' he said, keeping his voice low and reassuring. 'Act startled. You're not exactly sure where you're going, or why. Now there's a camp-fire. What in tarnation's that doing here? Then tears, maybe, as everything gets kinda muddled, the camp-fire, the other fire that's still smouldering a ways further south—'

'Enough, Cleet,' she said. 'We've been through all that.'

'And you're ready? No second thoughts?'

'Second thoughts, third thoughts, sure, there's those and more – but they all point me in the same direction: what I'm doing is right for Pete, right for Don Diego and Maria.'

There was the soft swish of metal on oiled leather as Sloan slipped his Winchester out of its boot. 'I've ridden this way several times, but night makes a fool of a man's memory. Cleet, you passed this camp just a couple of days ago. Can you recall what can be seen from that rise?'

'The cottonwoods and aspen get thinner up ahead where those fellers have been spreading their blankets.' He sucked his teeth. 'By the looks of it, that fire'll be brighter close up, and the moon will flood the small clearing with light. From up there, a man will see them clear as day.'

'Then we'll do it this way: I'll take the rise – looks like there's still some shadow below the skyline – you cut left, ride in along the river.'

Cleet nodded. 'The bank drops steeply, then flattens. The river's low this time of year, leaves a good strip of grass well clear of the gravel.'

'When we're in position, play it as it comes. Give Chrissy some time. If she can draw Waggoner and Blane away from the girl, see if you can work your way around and get close.' He looked at Chrissy, his face sombre. 'If Cleet manages to move in, he'll slip away into the woods with Maria while you've got Waggoner's and Blane's attention. That'll leave you in a hole. But up on that rise I'll be well placed to give covering fire. What I want you to do is to keep space between you and those two fellers; draw them away from Maria, but don't let them get too close to you. If I see Cleet getting away, I'll send a couple of shots whistling past those fellers' ears. Soon's I've got their attention, run like hell for the trees.'

'I'll point Maria in the right direction, make sure she's safe,' Cleet said, 'then come back. You'll have two of us covering you.'

'Chrissy . . .' Sloan stood in the stirrups, and Cleet saw him sweep the moonlit landscape with those sharp blue eyes that would miss nothing, looking right to the low rise, then traversing slowly left to where the moonlight transformed the river into a bright ribbon of silver. At that point he went still, and Cleet twisted in the saddle and looked towards the steeply sloping bank and across the glittering stretch of water to the flat grassland of Mexico.

Nothing moved. Detail faded as distance drained the light from the moon; shapes became shadows, shadows melted into darkness.

'Chrissy,' Sloan repeated, settling back in the saddle and turning to the girl, 'count slowly to five hundred, then ride in.' He hesitated. 'That pistol . . . I guess it makes you feel good, but against those fellers—'

'Last resort,' she said, her hand instinctively going to the hard outline under her jacket.

Her eyes were bright with excitement as she reached up to settle her black hat; the look she turned on Judson Cleet so charged with emotion that a lump came to his throat.

'With you two watching and me playing the maiden in distress, those fellers don't stand a chance,' she said. 'Now go on, move, both of you, or we'll be sitting here at sun-up.'

It turned out that Cleet had misread the ground at the edge of the river. Close up it was a mess of sparse grass and tufted weeds growing out of wet gravel. Under Rocky's hooves the small stones crackled like volleys from distant pistols, some of them shooting away to plop into deep water.

Hastily, Cleet edged the big horse closer to the high bank. The grass thickened, deadening the telltale sounds. But the ground rose towards the bank, and now his head and shoulders poked up into the moonlight. With a soft curse he tore off his battered, pale-grey Stetson and flipped it away, then ducked his head so that his face was in shadow.

As he peered from under his brows towards the rise, he could clearly see Marshal Sam Sloan moving his mount out of the trees and across the slope beneath the skyline. But that, Cleet knew, was because he was forewarned. From the campsite, any unsuspecting watcher's line of sight would be blocked by trees – and besides, if they were expecting the herd to cross the river at first light, they'd likely have their heads down.

Or maybe not both of them. One in his blankets, the other by the fire drinking coffee, smoking, idly watching the girl.

Maybe. Wait and see. Don't count chickens.

It got progressively trickier as his ride under the scant cover of the steep bank brought him level with the encampment. The trees some thirty yards from the river began to thin. Automatically counting along with Chrissy, Cleet had reached 400 when he got a good view of the fire – and knew that the reverse was true: from here on in he was dangerously exposed, and at least one man was awake. A figure was sitting hunched on the side of the fire away from the drifting smoke. Head down. Poking idly at the hanging black coffee pot with a stick. The flames lit up the white stetson, danced on the fancy tooled boots. Court Blane. And the man had only to turn his head . . .

A night bird rose into the air from the silent land across the river behind Cleet, big wings beating. Startled, the hair on his neck prickling, Cleet started, leaned forward to steady his horse, then froze. Blane

129

had caught the rhythmic sound of the bird's wings. Cleet ducked down, watched the big cattleman's head turn, from thirty yards away saw the firelight glinting in his eyes as he peered towards the river. As the sound of beating wings whispered into silence, Cleet sensed from the man's posture that he was suspicious; that he'd seen something, and was the kind who would worry at it like a dog with a bone. For several slow heartbeats the rancher remained still. Then he tossed the stick aside and came up from the log he'd been using as a seat, took a step away from the fire, his hand dropping to his six-gun – and, as he did so, Chrissy Moran came out of the trees and started her pony across the clearing.

Cleet let his breath out through his teeth in a soft hiss. He saw Blane pivot fast to face this new danger, saw the hand that had gone as a precaution to his holster now flick up and heard the sharp snap of the six-gun's cocking hammer.

'Waggoner!'

Chrissy was halfway across the clearing. Watching her steady approach, Blane yelled over his shoulder to Lupe Waggoner. Then he began backing away from the fire, keeping the veil of smoke between him and Chrissy as he retreated towards the trees. His eyes were everywhere, flicking away from the approaching rider to dart into the impenetrable shadows under the surrounding trees, cast by the rising moon and beyond the weak light of the flickering flames.

Movement snapped Cleet's eyes to the deeper shadows behind Blane. On a gentle slope at the edge of the trees he saw the shadowy shape of tethered horses, a huddled, blanket-covered form, the gleam of a pale face and the glint of light reflected in startled eyes. Then another figure was kicking blankets aside and coming erect in a flurry of crackling twigs. Tall, moving fast and with the warning flash of cold steel as he came erect, and Cleet knew the first figure was Maria Rivera, the second Lupe Waggoner.

He watched the drama unfold, and cursed softly.

They'd hoped the two men would advance to meet Chrissy, leaving Maria Rivera unattended. Instead, Court Blane continued to back steadily towards the trees while keeping the approaching rider covered, and Lupe Waggoner had drifted to the side to give him a clear line of fire without ever leaving the shadows, or the hostage.

Chrissy – bless her, thought Cleet! – saw what was happening and, remembering Sloan's advice, abruptly drew rein. She was still yards short of the fire. Her pony came to a halt, snorting softly. The girl folded her hands on the horn and swayed in the saddle. She remained that way, and suddenly the scene was a tableau frozen in time. It was as if even the necessary intakes of breath had been suspended, as if each person feared a wrong move would provoke a violent reaction that would overwhelm them.

Waggoner and Blane were motionless, dark shapes in deep shadow with pistols cocked, cattle rustlers waiting for a stolen herd to cross the Bravo and now

131

faced with uncertainty. Since the arrival of the Ranger, Pete Moran, Lupe Waggoner's every move had been watched, and killing Moran had only strengthened Sam Sloan's suspicions. Waggoner would surmise that, with his herd gone, Rivera would head for Old Town – but that would bring the law down on them, and now neither he nor Blane could figure out what was going on. In the silver light of the moon, wearing the serge jacket and flat black hat, Chrissy could be mistaken for a man. If that was the conclusion reached by the two nervous watchers, the long dark hair would create its own special fear. No lawman, this. Renegades? Indians? But if either, this silent rider was unlikely to be alone. Yet why was he bent and swaying in the saddle?

And it was like that, unanswered questions creating a deadly stand-off washed by cold moonlight with neither party willing to risk a move, when a rifle cracked behind Judson Cleet. Starting violently, he flattened himself in the saddle. A bullet whined wickedly, close enough to lift his hair, then slammed into the bank and kicked damp earth into his face.

Cleet was cursing himself for a careless fool as he flung himself from the saddle. The rifle cracked a second time. A bullet howled off a stone in a shower of sparks. He rolled tight up against the high bank, felt the healing shoulder wound tear, a stab of pain and the warm wetness of blood. Rocky trotted away with a shrill whinny and rattle of flying of stones.

Out of Cleet's sight, in the clearing, there was a sudden outburst of shouting and gunfire.

So intent had he been on watching Waggoner and Blane that the sounds of the river had been accepted by Cleet's subconscious as a part of the night that bore no threat. But the faint, lulling lap of water on gravel had been gradually pushed into the background by a swelling volume of sound that had gone unnoticed and now, as he looked, he saw the sullen water thrashed into moonlit white foam as two riders brought their wild-eyed mounts high-stepping with flashing hooves towards the edge of the Bravo.

A sombrero flapped madly above a grimacing face with one blind eye over a slashing scar. A black-clad devil built of skin and bone peered along a smoking rifle through sinister eyes as pale as moonlight. Even as Cleet stared in horror, that rifle spat flame and a bullet kicked dirt and left him spitting gravel. Then he'd sucked in a breath and was up and running. He lurched, his left shoulder scrubbing painfully against the bank. Bullets followed him, droning like deadly hornets. He risked a backward glance, saw Diaz and Van Haan splashing the last few yards to dry land.

Out of sight, a woman screamed.

Hard, racing footsteps approached rapidly. Suddenly, Lupe Waggoner was on the top of the bank, ten yards from Cleet, ice-blue eyes searching. Diaz's teeth flashed under his moustache as he roared, pointing. Waggoner's sprung-steel frame spun. He tilted his pistol, snapped it down and dropped the hammer. A bullet screamed towards Cleet. He felt it pluck at his sleeve. Another struck the bank, and he staggered. A flying stone clipped his cheek and drew blood. He ran, stumbling over wet gravel and clumped weeds, back muscles tightening as he waited for the bite of hot lead.

Then another rifle cracked, this one from the distant rise, and there was the deeper thump of a second, heavier weapon. Waggoner dropped flat. Diaz's horse screamed, then buckled at the knees. The Mexican spat out a rapid stream of Spanish expletives that was cut off as he splashed flat face down into shallow water suddenly topped with pink froth. Van Haan loosed a final wild shot into the distance then brought his horse out of the water and, in one mighty leap, up on to the high bank were Waggoner was grovelling for cover.

It gave Cleet time. Twenty yards, thirty, running hard, breath tearing at his throat. Then he was up with Rocky, standing with ears pricked and reins trailing in the water. He leaped into the saddle, flicked the reins and kicked hard with his heels. As the horse leaped forward and the wind began to sweep icily across Cleet's sweating face, he glanced swiftly back and across to take in the frantic action in the moonlit clearing.

Court Blane had run from the trees to leap the fire and was hanging on to taut reins as Chrissy tried to wheel her pony. She stretched out to lash wildly at the restraining hand with her quirt. The big man laughed.

He swung a massive fist at the pony's cheek, then grabbed for the mane. Waggoner was up on his feet. In a weaving run he crossed the clearing towards Blane and the girl. Sam Sloan's Winchester spat from the rise and kicked up the dirt in front of his dancing feet. A big buffalo gun boomed. Van Haan was hammering his horse towards the trees. Maria Rivera was out of her blankets, but dazed, weaving on unsteady legs. Diaz had dragged his Winchester from under the dead horse and splashed out of the water. Now, he was leaning up against the bank. With deadly, methodical precision he laid a series of aimed shots across the rise where Sam Sloan's Winchester and the unknown buffalo gun flashed fire.

Godammit! Cleet swung away, teeth clenched. Diaz and Van Haan back across the river ahead of the herd. Waggoner and Blane roused, and alert. And, unless Chrissy worked some magic, both girls now in the hands of the rustlers.

What seemed like hours ago Cleet had left Chrissy Moran and ridden at a leisurely pace to draw level with the camp to the slow count of 500. He made the return in a third of that time with the sound of gunfire dying out behind him, and brought Rocky to a wheeling, dust-flying stop at the edge of the broad trail where he had parted from Sloan and Chrissy. The dark, elegant figure of Don Diego Rivera eased his horse out of the shadows to greet him. As he did so, hoofbeats heralded the return of Sam Sloan.

'Yeah,' the marshal said drily to Cleet, as he drew

135

rein ahead of the big *vaquero*, Ramon, 'just like you said, everything was clear as day from the rise – and I can't believe how much good it did us!'

Chapter Fifteen

'What good will come of this madness?'

'*Dinero*,' said the Mexican, Diaz, and grinned wolfishly at Chrissy Moran.

From her blanket, Maria Rivera took one look at the ruffian's scarred face and milk-white eye and turned away, shuddering.

Between the clearing and the rise the horses making up the remuda were still restless: much of the firing had passed over their heads, and the thunder of the big Sharps and the hiss of flying bullets had driven them half wild. A short way from the trees the fire was crackling, spitting out sparks, smoke and flames from the fresh logs being tossed on by Johnny Van Haan. But the clearing was otherwise empty of life: Lupe Waggoner had herded the hostages out of the moonlight and under the trees, and the big cattleman and the Mexican who had been thrown into the water to come up stained with his dying horse's blood had both followed.

Now, Waggoner took over.

'I figured on one insurance policy,' he said. 'Now I've got two, and they'll see me all the way to Kansas.'

'Don't lay too much store on either one,' Chrissy said. Her face was white, and she cast frequent glances to the far side of the clearing where her pony lay dead in a pool of blood. 'Nobody'll be too concerned about a widow woman, and with Don Diego on the warpath, Maria's more trouble than she's worth.'

'On top of which,' said Van Haan, coming away from the fire with a thin black cheroot jutting from his teeth, 'we ain't going nowhere near Kansas. Last I heard, we ride with the herd as far as the Red, pocket the cash and head back to Fort Worth.'

'What cash?' said Court Blane.

'The cash,' Van Haan said, his pale eyes luminous, 'you handed over to Waggoner.'

Blane laughed. 'He tell you that?'

'You sayin' you didn't do it?'

'The only cash I know of is on the hoof. My deal with Waggoner is he buys steers for a couple of dollars a head, I take them north, we split the takings sixty-forty when we get to Ellsworth.'

'Well now,' Van Haan said softly. He struck a match, applied it to the cheroot, blew a stream of pungent smoke and grinned across at Waggoner. 'So which one of you's a liar, Lupe?'

The lean man snorted. 'What's the difference? Buy steers, steal 'em; take them to Ellsworth instead of the

Red; raise hell in Abilene 'stead of Forth Worth. One cow-town's as good—'

'Difference is,' said Van Haan, 'if you've got the habit you'll lie again, and again.'

'And maybe,' said Diaz, hunkered against a tree, 'we work our cojones off an' don' get no *dinero*.'

Waggoner looked at the two gunslingers, his cold blue eyes speculative. 'Where's Concho and the kid?'

Diaz spat. 'Don' worry about them. I see them shake hands with a few bottles, spend some time sleeping—'

'If that's true,' Waggoner said, 'it looks like you two get double wages at the end of the drive.' He lifted an eyebrow. 'Feel better?'

'Don't believe him,' said Chrissy, then fell back with a cry as the lean man's hand cut across her cheek with a whip-like crack and blood trickled from a split lip.

Maria Rivera whimpered softly.

Court Blane shook his head, stamped over to the fire and poured himself a cup of coffee. Van Haan watched him, flicked ash from the cheroot and a thin flicker of derision crossed his face.

'Lupe, it seems to me you two ain't entirely in agreement.'

Waggoner was wiping a smear of blood off the back of his hand. 'My partner brought his Houston gentleman's ethics all the way to southern Texas and got them dragged through the dust.'

Van Haan laughed. 'Found he's part owner of a stolen herd?'

'Not yet I'm not,' Blane growled, coming away from

the fire. 'I want you to let those girls go free.'

'And if I don't?'

Blane glared at Van Haan, a challenge in his penetrating gaze. 'I hear you lost two men. You reckon three of you can move those steers all the way to Kansas?'

Waggoner cocked his head. 'I'll answer that one with another question: if you walk away, why should your men go with you?'

'They're in my employ. They do what I say.'

'But when was their last pay day? Financially, you're on your knees, you make this drive or go under. If there's cash at the end of the trail, I reckon more than half of your men would ride with me.' His pale eyes bored into the cattleman. 'No matter how we got hold of those steers, circumstances are forcing you to accept a Kansas pay check – and you know we'll make it: Sam Sloan's the only lawman in five-hundred square miles, and once we hit the Chisholm nobody'll give the herd a second glance.'

'All right. Maybe I'm stuck with this drive. Maybe. But if it's going to be as easy as you say, leave the girls behind.'

Chrissy had walked away from the men and was sitting with her arm around Maria Rivera. Diaz had tipped his sombrero over his face and seemed to be asleep. Van Haan wandered over to the fire and sat down on the log, every now and then glancing towards the river as if listening.

Waggoner drew a breath, let it out.

'That was Judson Cleet down by the river. J.C. Cleet. Shootist—'

140

'He's mine,' Van Haan said. 'We'll see what kind of a shootist—'

'One of the fellers blasting from the rise,' Waggoner cut in impatiently, 'was Marshal Sam Sloan. Johnny, you seen anyone with a buffalo gun?'

'*Vaquero*, as big as a house,' Van Haan said. 'Alongside Rivera at Buena Vista.'

'Then that was him on the rise with Sloan,' Waggoner said, 'and Rivera won't be too far away.'

'Get to the point,' Blane said, nursing the hot cup of coffee.

'Once we hit the Chisholm, everything's rosy. But right now we've got four angry men watching us, and a herd to get across the Bravo. You think they won't use those long guns to pick us off?'

'Maybe. But you brought gunnies to fight off attacks by Indians and renegades. Why don't you use them for that purpose? Having that girl as hostage didn't stop Sloan and his friends tonight, and it won't stop them at dawn.'

From under the sombrero, Diaz said lazily, 'It will stop them, and without a fight. In daylight, if they get close and see me hold my knife to the *señorita*'s throat, they will back off.'

'And it's less than three hours to first light,' Waggoner told Blane. 'That's when your man Clayton will bring the herd across – so tell me now: are you in, or out?'

Dispirited by failure, aware that any daylight assault

would be more difficult and a long way from agreeing on tactics, they were nevertheless desperate to make some kind of move when the 'punchers were bringing the herd across the Bravo. With time to spare they tethered the horses and spread their blankets to sleep fitfully, drifting off time and again only to come awake with a start. The familiar night sounds were reassuring – the breeze whispering in the trees, the crackle of movement in thick brush, the mournful, keening cry of some far off animal – but each man knew that, all too soon, those sounds would be interrupted then drowned by the bawling of more than 2,000 steers, the hoarse cries of weary 'punchers moving sluggishly up the west bank of the Bravo.

Ramon heard them first, clambering out of his blankets to squint up at skies that had lightened while the four men dozed, then turning towards the south and west to where the high column of dust was already being picked out by a sun still well below the eastern horizon.

By the time the big lead steer had brought the herd level and the point riders were swinging it towards the river as most of the other 'punchers worked their way to the inland side of the herd, Sloan, Cleet, Rivera and Ramon had freshened up, methodically chewed on a breakfast of tough dry jerky eaten standing up and washed down with cold water, and checked their weapons.

All the while they stayed well back in the trees and kept a wary eye on the carefully controlled activity

142

across the river. Jack Clayton, Blane's strawboss, was easily picked out, skilfully directing operations from his constantly moving horse, ensuring that weary but thirsty cattle were held back until the 'punchers were in position and ready for the crossing, frequently looking across the river to where Cleet guessed Waggoner and Blane would be watching impatiently from a few hundred yards up the east bank. The cries of cattle and men drifted to them across the flat expanse of water. When the wind shifted, sounds were carried to them with a clarity that meant occasional words could be picked out. Dust rolled across the river in clouds, bringing with it the stink of sweating cattle that was thick and strong enough to chew.

But Cleet had been wrong about Blane.

'Rider coming!'

They had been watching from cover, and Sloan's sharp warning drove them deeper into the trees as they drew their six-guns. And, Cleet thought with amusement, it was a morning for wrong guesses: the man was off his horse and leading it, walking it off the trail on the grass close to the trees and scrub, his hand up close to the bit and his whole attention directed behind him.

He blundered straight on to Cleet's pistol barrel as the shootist stepped in front of him.

'Jesus Christ!'

'Good morning, Mr Blane.'

The big rancher recklessly pushed the pistol to one side.

'Don't be so damn stupid. I came looking for you.'

'Well, now, maybe we had you figured wrong.' This was Sloan, stepping out of the trees with a muttered curse as a the stub of a broken branch snagged his shirt. He tilted his six-gun and lowered the hammer, but circumspectly kept the weapon in his big fist.

Blane noted the action, and his smile was withering. 'I told you, there's no need for guns. I admit it: I was wrong from the outset, should have listened to you instead of Waggoner.'

'Glory be!' Cleet said. 'Is this the break we've been looking for?'

'I've opted for bankruptcy by walking out on a Kansas pay day,' the cattleman said. 'That leaves me facing ruin, but makes the odds against you marginally more favourable.' To Sloan, he added, 'They'd improved before I left: two of Waggoner's men – a kid with a harmonica and a man called Concho – stayed in Mexico to drown themselves in the local wine.'

Rivera stepped forward, his manner dignified, but tense. 'They are welcome to it, if it keeps them out of this ungodly mess. But you, sir, you have been close to my daughter. You can tell me if she is well – and what they intend doing with her?'

'You know damn near as much as I do. She's unharmed, but Diaz intends keeping you at bay by holding a knife to her throat. I walked out because I can't stomach such actions – and on the way I realized I could not bring myself to cross Texas with cattle stolen from your ranch.'

He looked to where Ramon was untying the horses, then away to the haze of dust drifting across the river and through it to where the first steers were approaching the water. He shook his head. 'My men will give you no trouble. They think I bought that herd, it's mine to sell. I'm sure they'll follow my lead when they learn the truth.' He looked at Sloan. 'How many men have you got?'

'What you see.'

Blane took a breath. 'Not enough – but those hostages mean your hands are tied anyway.'

'But against just three men,' Cleet said, 'there must be a way.'

He had been half listening, his mind absorbing what Blane was saying and quickly dismissing most of it as irrelevant or worthless. It was interesting to hear they were facing just Waggoner, Diaz and Van Haan, but even that helped little if one of those men was determined to stick close to at least one of the girls.

He strolled a short way away from the group, stopped under a tree to fire up a cigarette, absently heard Sloan telling Ramon to leave the horses where they were, they'd be going in on foot. There was a brief argument, and Cleet stood waiting as the marshal patted Don Diego on the shoulder and came across to join him.

'The way I see it,' Cleet said, 'is a nice, noisy diversion while one man sneaks in behind Diaz – if it's him – and frees the girls.'

'Same as last night,' Sloan said, clearly unimpressed. 'If it didn't work in darkness, what chance is there in daylight?'

'More going on. Easier targets for you and Ramon—'

'Me and Ramon?'

'I'm sneakier,' Cleet said, and grinned.

'I'll defer to your greater stealth,' Sloan said. 'So now I tell Ramon he does need his horse after all.'

'You're putting him on the ridge?'

'He's got a bigger gun.' And now it was Sloan's turn to grin.

'Ramon on the ridge with the Sharps,' Cleet said. 'That leaves you where?'

'One way to find out.'

He stepped away, called Blane over, and the two men spoke briefly. When Sloan rejoined Cleet he was thoughtful.

'Nothing's changed, according to Blane. They'll most likely keep Chrissy and Maria in the trees on the far side of the clearing. If Ramon's on the rise, I'll approach the clearing from this side. That leaves you to work your way around and come in behind whoever's with the girls.'

'Diaz.'

'Yeah. According to Blane. I reckon Waggoner will be interested in the herd. That leaves Van Haan. Odds of three against two, in our favour.'

'Made worthless by Diaz and the girls.'

'Which is something we work around.' Sloan pulled his corn-cob pipe out of his pocket, sucked on it, pulled a face and spat. 'What about Don Diego and Blane?'

146

'You tell me, Marshal.'

'Leave them well out of it?'

'Yeah. Too much sentiment on one side, resentment on the other. Last thing we want is amateurs lettin' their feelings take over.'

Sloan's eyes were amused. 'About as bad,' he said, 'as pinning hopes on a man who's spent the last few years drinking himself into boot-hill.'

'Are you finished,' Cleet said, 'or do you plan on talking all day?'

'Ready,' Sloan said.

'Then let's get this done.'

Chapter Sixteen

The rising sun was high enough for its dazzling rays to brush the shifting forest of glistening horns with streaks of fire when the steers were finally driven into the Bravo and the west bank became a muddy quagmire down which the animals slipped and slithered into water quickly churned into dirty brown foam.

Once on the move, the column turned and tumbled down the bank in a broad wave of sleek bodies and slashing, clicking horns. The slow-moving line that had been but a few animals deep became a rush impelled by panic. Steers at the back pushed blindly, relentlessly; those at the front that hesitated were driven into the water by the weight of bodies, many bawling plaintively as they went down and were trampled.

In the water, heads high, nostrils flaring beneath rolling eyes, steers began to drift with the deceptively strong current. Dust was a choking cloud over dun-coloured water torn ragged. 'Punchers yipped shrilly, lashed out with coiled ropes, and tried to keep the steers upstream when they were not themselves thrown from the saddle to cling to the horn and swim alongside their horses.

It was with that backdrop of incessant noise as a constant reminder of what was happening around him that Judson Cleet, bone-handled six-guns snug on his thighs, worked his way with a trapper's care through the trees bordering the clearing.

Ramon had already left, armed with his big Sharps .50, his swarthy face set but the light of battle dancing in his black eyes as he rode a wide loop that would take him to his vantage point on the rise.

Sam Sloan was behind Cleet, following a straight path through the trees to the clearing's near edge. He would be in position first, and would then wait for the first, booming report from the big *vaquero*'s buffalo gun.

When that shot came, Cleet had to be in position.

Despite the covering noise of the herd fighting its way across the Bravo, every time a branch snapped under a lowered boot Cleet winced and waited for the warning shout, the crack of a pistol; each time a break in the trees left him dangerously exposed he darted across the gap at a crouching run then forced himself to stop, catch his breath, and test the air. Those pauses brought with them the prickle of cold sweat. Tension mounted to an unbearable pitch, turning his muscles into tight knots as every nerve screamed at him to drop caution and push on recklessly. Ramon, mounted, would rapidly gain his vantage point, and begin counting the minutes to when he would fire his first, carefully aimed shot. Time was running out for Cleet – yet he had no doubts about the enormity of his task, or of the deadly ability of the two gunslingers, Diaz and Van Haan. The men were seasoned owlhoots. They were alive today because they had honed the ability to stay alert even when bone-weary and one jump ahead of a chasing posse. And if the Mexican, Diaz, had been given the dangerous task of sticking close to Maria Rivera, then Waggoner and Van Haan would be able to take up positions elsewhere, and watch for Cleet from cover.

For Cleet had no doubt it was him they would be expecting. When the two waddies, Burke and Riley had picked a fight with him in the saloon – God! how many long days ago? – it was because Lupe Waggoner had sensed instinctively that Cleet was the danger. That instinct had been proved correct. Burke and Riley had been killed. The second attempt on Cleet's life had failed. And Cleet knew that this time it would be the black-clad, vengeful gunslinger Johnny Van Haan who would step out into the morning sun with his black-gloved hand poised over the six-gun pouched butt first on his left hip.

He would watch from cover. His challenge would come in the open. For one of them – the slow one – it would end in death.

It was Diaz.

Still working his way stealthily north through the

woods, Cleet reached another gap and ducked down to look towards the river. At once, he saw the two hostages. They were standing with the Mexican some fifty yards away, by an untidy sprawl of blankets at the northern edge of the trees close to the dying camp-fire. And Cleet was down on one knee in the scrub, studying the situation and the immediate area through narrowed eyes, calculating how much further he had to walk to come back through the woods behind the Mexican, when Ramon's big rifle boomed.

The bullet hissed across the clearing, and smacked into a rock close to the river bank. From the other side of that steep bank Cleet knew so well, a rifle barrel poked up and spat flame. A second opened up from a similar position some thirty yards to the south; both gunmen were directing their fire at the rise.

Waggoner and Van Haan.

Caught flat-footed, in no-man's land, Cleet watched helplessly as Diaz sprang like a cat and grabbed Maria Rivera. She squealed. A blade flashed in the Mexican's hand. Then, his other arm hooked around her pale throat, Diaz wrestled the terrified girl through the trees into thick undergrowth.

Chrissy Moran turned, and looked directly at Cleet.

She had sensed his presence. Too far away, he was unable to read the message in her dark eyes. But as he took in the situation, a thrill of excitement coursed through him. The previous night's ruse had failed, but Chrissy was now in a unique position: Diaz had his hands full controlling the Mexican girl; Waggoner and

Van Haan were concentrating on Ramon, and it was as if all three men had ignored the possibility that Chrissy Moran might constitute a danger.

But what could she do?

Above the bawling of cattle and the cries of 'punchers, the detonations of the rifles at the river bank were staccato cracks punctuated by the spaced booms of Ramon's Sharps. But the big *vaquero* was untouchable: Waggoner and Van Haan were wasting ammunition. Cleet knew that Sam Sloan would be on the south fringe of the woods. He would have his Winchester at the ready, but his sharp blue eyes would be looking across the clearing as he waited for a signal from his deputy. He would expect Cleet to take Diaz, and emerge with the girl – but Cleet hadn't even made it that far.

There was too little time! It could not be long, surely, before Waggoner realized that Ramon's line of fire was severely restricted, and called off the futile exchange of shots? Not long, either, before he and Van Haan ran across to join Diaz and made the odds insurmountable.

Too little time – but what was left must be used.

Thinking had taken scant seconds. Chrissy was still out in the open, looking his way. Sweating, Cleet lifted a hand, rotated it to show that he would work his way around behind Diaz, saw her head dip in acknowledgement – and, at that moment, Don Diego Rivera ran into the clearing.

Damn, damn, damn! The man was supposed to be with Blane, looking after the horses!

The elderly *ranchero* ran doggedly, and in silence. His pace was slowed by the stiffness of age and a slight limp. But his face was a grey mask of determination, and in his lean fist a fancy six-gun jutted. His dark eyes were fixed on the smouldering fire, on Chrissy Moran – and, beyond her, the woods that completely concealed his daughter and her captor. His bravery was magnificent; his foolishness made disaster a certainty.

Cleet watched, horrified. He could do nothing. Diaz was many yards away; the knife he held needed to move but a few inches.

Then Chrissy acted. With a swift glance at the advancing *ranchero*, she turned her back on him and ran lightly across the blankets and into the woods.

For an instant, Cleet thought she'd lost her mind: she'd mistaken Rivera for one of the gunslingers, panicked, and run.

Then common sense took over, and with it came admiration. The girl knew that if Diaz could not be seen by those looking for him, it was unlikely that he could see clearly – and besides, she had always been between him and Rivera. So he would not yet know that the girl's father was charging towards him: he could not see him, the *ranchero* was advancing silently, and most sounds that morning were overwhelmed by the muted roar of the cattle and men crossing the Bravo.

And then, as that thought drew Cleet's gaze momentarily towards the river, he saw something that brought a delighted grin to his face: the first of the steers had crossed the Bravo and reached the east bank.

Waggoner and Van Haan were in a precarious position, trapped against the bank, with steers beginning to pour out of the river in an unstoppable flood. The shooting ceased abruptly. At the same time, a roar of pain came from the woods and Cleet was up on his feet and running.

Out of the corner of his eye he saw Sam Sloan coming after Rivera, then cutting left towards the river as Lupe Waggoner came up over the bank. Cleet cut in front of the *ranchero*, then leaped the dying fire and charged into the trees. Fifteen feet in through matted scrub, he saw Chrissy. She was holding a thick branch, gripping it tightly in both her hands like a club. Diaz's knife lay glittering at her feet. Beyond her, the Mexican's face was twisted with pain, his right hand broken and limp – but in his left hand he held a cocked pistol, and already it was swinging to bear on Chrissy.

Cleet drew. As his hand went down it was if he relived every draw he had ever made, weighed the importance of each and found it wanting. The time that had been fast running out had run its course. Everything stood still, and nothing more still than Diaz. Cleet's draw was swift, lightning swift; Diaz had only to pull the trigger but was denied the fraction of the second he needed – and it was his last.

Cleet's bullet took the Mexican in the throat and knocked him backwards. He went down choking, died as his blood welled thick and red into the dead leaves. Chrissy dropped the branch, turned to Cleet and fell into his arms. She was shaking. He stroked her hair, looked over her head to where Maria cowered on the ground, face bone white, eyes dark and enormous.

Then Rivera was there, wheezing, the big fancy pistol up and wavering with the effort of his run as he searched for the target he craved but would have been unable to hit. And now there was no need. His shrewd old eyes saw the dead Mexican and flew to his daughter, and Cleet turned away as father and daughter came together with murmurs that were soft and broken with relief.

And then he left Chrissy.

'Sam's out there,' he said softly, and he touched her face gently and went back to the clearing.

Lupe Waggoner was down and dead, Sam Sloan spread legged with his pistol cocked and waiting as Johnny Van Haan came over the bank. The gunman was tall and lean and black against a backdrop of dust and milling steers slick with river water, the steam of their breath and their bodies clouding to mingle with dust and spray, their bellows cries of torment in a scene from Hades in which a grinning Van Haan played the Devil.

'Leave him,' Cleet called to Sloan.

'The girls?'

'Safe.'

'Your doing?'

156

'Partly – but whatever else, this one's mine.'

And Van Haan was close enough to hear.

'Settling time,' he said, laughing. 'Time to even old scores.'

'I thought your brother was a sharp,' Cleet said, 'dealing cards off the bottom. What I did to him changed my life.'

'He fell in the sawdust in a rain of coloured chips, a kid who'd done nothing wrong.'

'He was with you.'

Again Van Haan laughed. 'Guilt by association? He was with me, so he cheated?'

'I was wrong. But I can't bring him back.'

'Then go join him,' Van Haan said, and went for his gun.

Did Cleet consciously allow the Lousiana man time to draw? Did he allow him that fraction of a second – the time denied to Diaz – and still beat him?

If Sam Sloan had been asked, he would have stated that the action was so fast nobody could tell for sure. And Judson Cleet? Well, he knew what he knew, and kept it to himself.

The cross draw looks awkward, but pulling a six-gun in that fashion is a sight easier than lifting one from a holster strapped on the same side. Van Haan's hand was a blur across his body. The .44 seemed to leap to meet it. Hand and six-gun flipped to the front. In that motion, the .44 was cocked.

And now – if you were to ask, and believe, Chrissy Moran – Judson Cleet made his move. If Van Haan's hand was a blur, Cleet's was beyond the range of human sight. The bone-handled six-gun was in its holster, then it spat flame; between one and the other there was no perceptible movement. And it was as if Van Haan was still making up his mind what to do with the six-gun that had appeared in his hand when Cleet's bullet took him in the chest.

The black-clad gunslinger went down where he stood, crumpling to the ground. Cleet went with him, following him down as if he was seeing once again the young kid with his pack of cards and the look of terror in his eyes. But in these older eyes the look was that of a devil with no regrets, and the mockery that lurked in their depths was put into words when Cleet leaned close.

'He lived another five years,' Van Haan whispered, through lips that wept blood.

'Your brother?'

A weak nod. 'Lived five years . . . then took a slug from the same man killed his ma and pa.'

'You!'

'A Lousiana man who went loco one time too many,' Van Haan said, and choked on a laugh. 'You changed your whole damn life for no reason, Cleet.'

He died as Cleet was absorbing the shock. It was a shock that took from an ageing gunslinger a weight that had pulled him down for too many long years, sent him drowning his regrets in a hundred border saloons.

And now?

Now he was free.

And when he turned to catch Chrissy Moran as she flung herself at him and, under the watchful eye of the grinning Sam Sloan, gathered her into his arms, in the eyes of that old gunslinger there might have been detected the faintest hint of unshed tears.

But about that, too, Sam Sloan would never be drawn.